SIRENS & SNOW

FINNELY RAY

Also By
FINNELY RAY

The Rosary's Reject's Series:
Demons & Museums
Angels & Exorcists

Short Fiction:
Let Down Your Hair - Voices of Romance: A Collective

WANT TO KNOW WHAT
SIRENS & SNOW
SOUNDS LIKE?

SCAN FOR SPOTIFY

SCAN FOR YOUTUBE

Author's Note

Sirens & Snow contains graphic violence and conversations surrounding intimate partner abuse, child death, homophobia and transphobia. Reader discretion is advised.

Mom – If you ever loved Grandma, do NOT read her this book.

Dad – Maybe sit this one out. Love you.

EMRYS HEMLOCK HATED ROUTINE. It was mortal bullshit designed to keep them distracted from the cosmic unknowingness of the universe, and he simply did not abide by it. But then he discovered that routine could include waking up to eat breakfast with Maryam Bishop (his roommate), flirting with Zackary Bishop (his other roommate), working at Ectoplasm: Coffee and Spirits, squabbling with Zackary, working the evening shift as well (because honestly, what else did he really have to do?), making a few more passes at Zackary, calling it a night and then doing the same thing all over again the next day. Then, and *only* then, did he find himself giving the concept of routine" a pass. This routine felt like a safe, warm den that smelled of coffee and sugar rather than a house of cards about to be toppled over by a bored god who felt like fucking with him. This routine felt like home.

Not that Emrys would ever say that out loud. He would rather swallow an iron nail.

Maryam's voice broke him out of his thoughts and brought him back to the morning rush. "Em, do you have that chai?"

"It's on your left." Emrys focused on the foam he was attempting to pour into the shape of a heart. It hardly mattered on to-go orders, given the lids, but he was determined to master it.

He silently wondered if he should be horrified at what he had become—this mundane little thing that liked routine and served mortals dirty chais with oat milk—and placed a lid on the coffee. As the cute customer smiled at Emrys, he decided it didn't matter.

Bright purple movement outside the front windows caught his attention. He watched as Alex, a fellow barista, sped-walked into the cafe, bundled from head to toe. Emrys shivered in the sudden sharp bite of February chill from the open door and longed for spring.

"Fuck, it's like *The Day After Tomorrow* out there." Alex peeled off their garments and shook off the flecks of melted snow and ice.

"Nah. Not enough people dying in the streets," Maryam chimed in.

Zackary flashed his goddaughter a dirty look over his laptop from his bar stool. "There are customers, Maryam Grace."

Maryam folded her arms. "That movie is almost as old as you are. Saying people die in it doesn't count as a spoiler."

"It's macabre and inappropriate," Zackary explained. Before Maryam could say anything even more macabre and inappropriate, he turned his attention to Alex. "Is something wrong? You're not on the schedule until tomorrow."

"I wanted to talk to you about that, actually." Alex brushed melted droplets from their purple hair. "Would you be okay if I switch with someone on Valentine's Day?"

Maryam leaned on the counter, one brow raised and eyes filled with mischief. "And why, pray tell, would *you* need Valentine's Day off?"

Alex bristled. "Did I indicate that it was any of your business?"

Maryam's smirk grew with the realization that she'd struck a nerve. "Doesn't matter. If you want *me* to take it, I want deets."

Alex turned to Emrys. "What about you?"

"Don't know yet." Emrys leaned on the counter across from Zackary. "*Someone* hasn't told me what our plans are yet."

Zackary began typing again, gaze focused on the screen. "That's because *someone* will be busy with a bar full of awkward first dates and lonely people looking to score thanks to this gaudy, insufferable holiday. The emergency rideshares aren't going to call themselves. Besides, that's your night to close, remember?"

"Fine by me." Emrys tipped Zackary's screen forward so the demon couldn't see the contents. "What are we doing afterward?"

"Going to bed."

"Together?"

Zackary gave Emrys a sickly-sweet smile as he gently pried Emrys' fingers off his computer and opened the screen again. "I'll treat you to a nice cup of tea, and you can tell me all about your day. How about that?"

Emrys bristled. Months ago, when Zackary said that he was going to flirt sweetly whenever Emrys flirted dirty, he had expected him to give up after a day or two. Four months later, Zackary was still at it, meeting Emrys' advances with sugar more often than barbs, throwing the pixie off-balance and sending his heart racing.

It was disgusting.

Emrys scoffed. "Gods. Why are you such an old man?"

"Don't know. Why won't you let me take you out to dinner?"

Emrys glared and turned to Alex, not wanting to give Zackary the satisfaction of a reply. "Sorry, love. Looks like I'm on the schedule already."

"Now, this is going to sound crazy," Maryam interjected. "But you could try talking to an employee here who *isn't* me or Emrys. Pretty sure the rest of the staff thinks you're mute."

Alex groaned, then shoved their hands in their pockets. "Fine. Take my shift. I'll text you tonight."

Maryam let out a victorious "*Yessss*" under her breath as she gave a victorious fist pump.

Alex checked their phone and headed back for the door. "Repeat anything I tell you, and I'm hexing the shit out of you and your firstborn."

Maryam snorted. "Joke's on you—I'm not having kids."

"Tell that to the hex." Alex held the door for a pair of customers, then disappeared into the blustery Detroit cityscape. Maryam welcomed the newcomers with a smile and asked if they'd been to Ectoplasm before, leaving Emrys to watch Zackary as he continued to work.

The demon had grown less reclusive in the months since Emrys had conned his way into the Bishop household. More often than not these days, Zackary would work at the bar, provided the place wasn't nearing maximum capacity. Emrys could hardly take all the credit, though. On the heels of Emrys crashing into his and Maryam's life, their neighbor Peter had ended up with a particularly nasty demon haunting his apartment. Rarely capable of doing what she was told, Maryam went looking to help and stumbled upon the fact that she was half-demon. Ankida'shi, as Zackary called it. Zackary's boss and wrangler, the Rosary Order, not only didn't care for demons, but they didn't care for half-demons either. Between the bad demon (Peter's), the good demon (Zackary), and the half-demon (Maryam), a lot of nastiness had ensued. Still, as far as Emrys could tell, it had ended well, leaving everyone lighter and freer, thanks to the magic of the truth, or whatever the bullshit cliché was. He'd heard Maryam wake up screaming more than once since then, but she'd be fine. Eventually. Hopefully.

"Keep staring at me, and I'm writing you up for harassment," Zackary said without missing a keystroke.

Emrys snorted. "I wasn't staring at you."

Zackary gave him a doubtful look.

"I was gazing forlornly. There's a difference."

A ghost of a grin crept onto Zackary's face as he continued to work.

That was the first genuine smile Emrys had seen from him all day. Something about being the one to draw it from him sent butterflies fluttering through his stomach, making him giddy and nauseous in equal measure, which was annoying. He wasn't supposed to feel any of those things—he was supposed to get Zackary into bed, where Emrys could tangle those strawberry-blonde waves in his hands as the demon did all sorts of unholy things to him with that chiseled body.

But that wasn't about to happen on the clock, so Emrys took a rag from a bucket of sudsy water below the bar and began wiping down the counter.

"Do you really think Valentine's Day is gaudy and insufferable?" he asked.

"I suppose not." Zackary sat back, arms crossed, as he studied the screen and ran his thumb back and forth across his chin. "I guess I've always known love to be a quiet thing. While I suppose there's nothing wrong with loud, exuberant displays to demonstrate it, I feel like it cheapens it a bit." He shrugged and went back to typing. "That's just me, though."

Emrys smirked. "Okay, but what if there was a *good* reason for Valentine's Day to get loud?"

Zackary flashed him a dirty look. His gaze slipped past Emrys and locked on the front door, his expression shifting to confusion. "Father Wilhelm?"

Emrys turned. He didn't know a Wilhelm, but anyone called "Father" was bound to be from the Rosary Order, meaning this visit was work-related, which was alarming. Ectoplasm and the Rosary Order were worlds never meant to mix, from what he could tell.

The classic black cassock gave Father Wilhelm away among the customers. He was an older white man with a hollowing face and wispy straw-blonde hair that seemed to almost frame his head like a halo when he removed his hat. His dark eyes were bright, and his smile beaming, revealing a youthful, vibrant soul underneath.

Emrys couldn't help but wonder what he might find if he whisked Wilhelm off to Faerieland. After a few days of eating faerie food and drinking faerie wine, the priest might very well be a looker—one Emrys would be more than happy to show a good time if he didn't let a pesky thing like vows of chastity get in the way.

"Afternoon, Zackary." The priest removed his bright red scarf with a hint of a chuckle as he stood in Zackary's stunned silence. "Don't look so excited to see me."

Zackary shut his laptop, along with his slightly agape mouth, and slid off the bar stool. "Sorry. It's always a pleasure, but I don't think anyone from the Order has ever paid us a visit before."

"Oh, I did several months ago," Father Wilhelm said. "I delivered a letter to Maryam apologizing for the Order's mistreatment of her and offering her a job in our ranks."

Zackary scowled toward his goddaughter, who was bussing a table at the other end of the bar. "Funny. She's never mentioned that before."

Oh, no." The priest chuckled. "I didn't get her in trouble, did I?"

"Well, if you didn't, she'd find a way into it on her own." Zackary sighed. "What can I do for you, Father?"

"A rather unique case came in this morning," Father Wilhelm said. "One I think you two would be uniquely capable of handling."

Zackary's eyebrows raised. "You mean me and Maryam?" He folded his arms. "Getting her to help me on cases is like pulling teeth, so it may be a hard sell coming from you, Father. No offense."

"None taken, but Maryam's not who I'm talking about." Father Wilhelm's gaze fell on Emrys with a curiously mischievous glint. "I'm talking about Mr. Hemlock here."

Zackary watched as Emrys' eyebrows shoot up. The pixie covered a laugh with a weak cough so as not to be rude. "So sorry. I don't think I heard you right." It took several attempts to get more words out, as if Emrys couldn't find the right way to string them together. "You said that you, a priest from the Rosary Order, need to speak to *me*?"

"The both of you, yes." Father Wilhelm glanced around the bustling cafe. "Is there somewhere we can speak privately by chance?"

"Of course." Zackary motioned toward his office. "If you would follow me, Father." He held the office door open for both Father Wilhelm and Emrys, who still looked bewildered. Normally, Zackary would savor any instance of Emrys being thrown off-kilter, but he wasn't particularly comfortable with the priest's request himself. He gestured to the rickety rolling chair before his equally rickety desk and ancient computer, self-conscious of the sad state of the amenities he used in order to avoid working out of the Order. "Would you like a seat, Father?"

Father Wilhelm gave a slight wave of dismissal. "No, that's quite alright. I sit entirely too much back in my study." He placed his briefcase on the desk, opened it, and shuffled through papers. "A local case came in yesterday that I thought you two would be uniquely equipped to handle." He handed Zackary a cream-colored folder. "I say local, but it's all the way in the Upper Peninsula." The priest frowned. "Brace yourselves. The images aren't pretty."

Zackary opened the folder with little bracing. Judging by the way Emrys placed a hand on Zackary's arm for balance, standing on his toes and eagerly craning his neck to peer at the contents, he wasn't about to be fazed either. Zackary removed the paper-clipped contents and flipped through police reports, personal statements, and Order correspondence.

"The first victim is named Collin Franklin," Father Wilhelm began. "Nineteen years old. Born and raised in the village of Glace, Michigan, where his body was found. He lived at home while he worked toward an automotive certification. A local woman was walking her dog around seven in the morning three days ago when she found his body washed up on the beach. She thought he was a mannequin until she got close enough to recognize him."

Zackary flipped to an image of a lifeless body on a metal slab—the former Collin Franklin—and his stomach lurched. Nineteen looked so much younger when it had been cut short, possibly by the ice-cold water of Lake Superior, judging by the milky blue tint of Collin's skin and the purple hue of his lips. His blond hair, still shaggy with adolescence, alternated between being plastered to his forehead and sticking out at odd angles, as if the poor kid had just fallen asleep after a swim.

Zackary's gaze caught on dark markings along Collin's neck and collarbone before he could flip to another page. He looked closer, his face twisting in disgust. "Are those *bite marks*?"

"And hickeys, I think." Emrys craned his arm around Zackary's to point at small nondescript bruises in the same area.

Zackary looked closer and cringed as he decided he might be right.

"The coroner thinks those must have happened within six hours of the boy's death," Father Wilhelm said.

"Did he have a romantic partner?" Zackary asked.

"A girlfriend, but she's at school in Grand Rapids. She was out with friends until ten that night. Collin's parents said he went up to bed around the same time. Even if she left town exactly at ten and drove all night, she wouldn't reach Glace until about five in the morning."

Emrys gave an indignant snort as he dropped his arm. "That doesn't necessarily answer the question, Father."

Father Wilhelm raised an eyebrow at him. "Collin's phone was searched. There was no indication that he was seeing anyone else. Besides, he was found in an oversized T-shirt, basketball shorts, and no socks. If he was stepping out on his girlfriend in the middle of winter, I imagine he would have wanted more clothes."

Zackary flipped through more pages, trying to ignore the way Emrys stared down the priest with a glare. He discovered the second set of images—another young man, likely Collin's age, with dark curly hair and a heavier build with the same bleach-blue skin and marks.

"That's Ian Phillips," Father Wilhelm chimed in. "He's reported to be one of Collin's oldest friends and was found yesterday morning in the exact same spot." Father Wilhelm's face sobered. "The boys' parents reported they were acting strange in the weeks leading up to their deaths. It started small—sleeping with hall lights on and asking if anyone else could hear singing at night. They grew reclusive, calling in sick to work and school to hide. From what, we can't say. When the police went to their houses to look for clues, both their rooms were locked from the inside. Windows, too. Both families have cameras on their front porches. No one came in or out all night."

"Any history of drug use? Mental illness?"

Father Wilhelm shook his head. "Not on either account. And the toxicology report didn't show anything in their systems. According to the autopsy, they drowned, but they were perfectly healthy the nights they died."

Zackary studied Ian Phillips' body again, his chest aching with the thought of how much fear the young man must have felt, and his parents' agony upon realizing that their son was never going to walk out of his bedroom again.

Echoes of his own agony shot through his body, along with its own grotesque images.

Zackary snapped the file shut. "What are the police saying?"

They think it was planned. Organized. Either they're looking for a single suspect or a single group of suspects." Father Wilhelm massaged his temple. The Chief of Police suggested cult activity in an interview, and we really wish he hadn't. There's a small local witch coven who our informant is now worried about. They're harmless neo-pagans, but Glace is small. Conservative. Religious. Thanks to that Chief, whispers are starting that the witches put a curse on the boys. Collin's father is the pastor of the largest congregation in town, and both boys were highly active in the church. The story goes that the boys tried to minister to the witches, but they didn't take too kindly to it and called on Satan and his demons to attack them." He snapped his briefcase closed; his grip still tense. "It's nonsense, of course, but the informant's worried. Apparently, more than one person has started getting nasty with them. She's worried that if we don't step in before there's another murder, mob rule will start to take over."

Emrys raised an eyebrow. "The Rosary Order has informants?"

Father Wilhelm nodded. "Of sorts. Her name is Gracie Quill. She was a member of the Order but left in the early seventies for personal reasons." Father Wilhelm removed his glasses and polished them with his scarf. "I was actually quite surprised to hear from her. This is the first time she's reached out since she left."

Zackary began to flip through the papers a second time. What do you think it is, Father?

He placed the glasses back on his long nose, his gaze burning into both Zackary and Emrys. "Between the singing, the drowning, and the bruises, I believe it was a siren."

Emrys stood still, arms folded comfortably, his weight more on his right foot than his left, head tilted a bit to the side. It was a stance Zackary had seen a hundred times when the wheels in Emrys' mind were spinning particularly fast, but Zackary had never felt dread radiate off him like this before. He practically vibrated with it.

"So, will you take the case? The both of you?" Desperation seeped into the old priest's voice.

Zackary answered, "Of course," at the same time Emrys answered, "I can't."

Zackary whirled on him. "What do you mean you can't?"

"What do you mean, *what do you mean you can't?*" Emrys fired back, dropping his voice low and mocking. "I'm not an exorcist. I'm not coming. Take Maryam."

Zackary glowered. Eyes still locked on Emrys, he said, "Would you give us the room, Father?"

Father Wilhelm nodded. He folded his hands in front of him as he began walking toward the office door. "Of course."

"Thank you." Zackary leaned against his desk, ankles and arms crossed, his gaze fixed on Emrys as the pixie glared back, hackles raised like a spooked stray cat. "Help yourself to a coffee and something from the pastry case. My treat."

"That's very kind of you."

The door clicked shut. Zackary still waited, trying to decide how best to approach Emrys' abrupt change in mood.

He settled on, "What the hell's gotten into you?"

"Nothing, you old gargoyle." Emrys unfolded his arms, holding them wide as though to prove he had nothing to hide.

"Don't lie to me, Emrys."

Emrys snorted. "Faeries can't lie."

"No, but they can bullshit." Zackary studied Emrys, the way he couldn't hold Zackary's gaze. The way he didn't seem to know what to do with his hands—wringing them, swinging his arms, then playing with the loops of his jeans. "When Father Wilhelm said that a siren had killed the boys, that scared you. Why." It wasn't a question.

Emrys scoffed. "I was not *scared.*"

"You're right—you were terrified. I could practically smell it on you."

Emrys opened his mouth to argue.

Zackary cut him off. "Spare me. Spill it." Still nothing. Zackary scowled. "I'm going whether you come or not. Do you really want me to walk in there blind?"

Emrys' lips pursed together, his brow furrowed as if he were struggling to keep his mouth shut. He let out a defeated puff of breath, running a hand over his hair, letting it fall in his face, and then massaging the back of his neck. "Fine." He kept his gaze on the walls. The floor. The door. The computer. Anywhere but Zackary. "I was...*with* a siren some years back. Fifty, maybe? Sixty? They're dark folk. Not twilight and dawn like most faeries. *Dark.* Dark as an ocean trench and twice as deadly." He shivered, bringing his arms around himself as if he could stave off a chill.

Zackary watched, alarms sounding in his head. Emrys didn't get small like this. He didn't curl in on himself and shrink. His sense of self-preservation was dangerously in short supply normally, not kicked into overdrive. So what had happened to him all those years ago, and how severely did Zackary have to punish this siren after dragging them in for murder? "Emrys...did they—"

"No." The word was fast. Clipped. Too insistent. Emrys shook his head. "No, she didn't. She was just..." He shook his head again, then raised his gaze to Zackary, those azure orbs pleading and desperate. "It's not even the same siren. It can't be. My partner never liked mingling with mortals but, whoever it is, they're going to be dangerous, and I'm not strong."

Zackary blinked, a hint of a smile twitching his lips. "Is that seriously what you're worried about? All this because you're not *strong*?"

Emrys shot Zackary a nasty look filled with enough venom to wither a full-grown tree. He unfolded his arms and marched toward the door, shoulder-checking Zackary on his way. "Eat shit, Zackary."

Zackary barely felt the strike. He gently grabbed Emrys' slender arm before he could escape, his grip nearly circling Emrys' bicep. "Wait."

Emrys scowled up at him, a barb ready on his tongue, no doubt.

Zackary met his gaze, refusing to blink. "You are more than strong. You are smart. You are resilient and quick thinking and clever—"

Emrys scoffed with a roll of his eyes. "It's a little late to butter me up—"

"I mean it." He did his best to soften his body language as he silently kicked himself. Emrys wasn't like Maryam. He wasn't like the mortals he worked with at the Order or the demons and Ankida'shi at the dawn of time. Truth be told, even after four months, Zackary wasn't quite sure if he could fully pin down *what* Emrys was like. He hid behind too many walls. Too many crude jokes and sexual offers. Too much bright laughter and deceivingly high spirits.

Despite himself, Zackary desperately wanted to know what Emrys hid behind those walls, no matter how hard Emrys tried to keep him out. No matter what a fool that might make him—what a fool it *did* make him.

He sighed and loosened his grip. "I need you on this, Em. I'm a bumbling idiot when it comes to the goodfolk, and you know it. I can't stop this without you."

The pixie's gaze darted over the demon's face, his blue eyes calculating and unsure. "You can be a heavy-handed prick sometimes," he snapped. "Did you know that?"

"I did." Zackary released him. "I'm sorry." He waited for an accep-tance that did not come. "You don't have to face this. Tell me how to take down a siren and I'll handle it from there."

Emrys' lips pursed, his eyebrows pulling together to form a valley of worry against his forehead.

Zackary did his best not to groan with preemptive regret as he went to his last resort. "Do this for me, and you get me to yourself for a whole day. Nothing, except sex, is off-limits."

Emrys blinked, his eyebrows disappearing beneath his wavy hair, mischief back in his eyes. "Truly nothing?"

"Nothing that breaks the law or involves intercourse. Everything else is on the table."

Emrys pulled away and smirked, looking Zackary up and down. "If that's the case..." He held out his hand. "We have a deal."

"No deal." The demon folded his arms to drive his point home. "We're doing this as partners. Friends. If you ever get too uncomfort-able, you're allowed to pull out—"

"Not something I generally have to worry about."

Zackary glared Emrys into silence. I'm not going to cage you in with a magical contract."

The pixie dropped his hand and sighed. "Fine. Your call, boss."

Zackary cringed. "Don't call me that."

"Sure thing, daddy."

"Stop. Before I change my mind."

"You won't." Emrys strolled toward the door. "You *need* me, re-member?" He flashed Zackary one last smirk and a wink before push-ing it open to the cafe.

Zackary ground his teeth, furious with himself for thinking he could show a moment of vulnerability without Emrys throwing it back in his face as a joke.

Worse, he was angry because Emrys was right: Zackary needed him.

Emrys' 3:00 am alarm annihilated his giddy anticipation for the trip. He rolled from his cot in the apartment's front closet, tossed his haphazardly stuffed backpack onto the sofa , and went through the motions of getting breakfast without a single glimmer of consciousness. Zackary operated in his usual militant efficiency, reading the case file for the fifth time over his coffee, then triple-checking the flight details on his phone. The only coherent thought Emrys could muster was gratitude that the demon knew not to talk this early.

The biting, blistery cold of the dark Detroit morning helped a bit. By the time Father Wilhelm drove up in an old beat-up compact car, Emrys could string together a mumbly "Good morning" as he crawled into the back.

The priest passed him a large fastened envelope between the seats. "Congratulations, you're a real human person now. Everything you need, should any questions arise, is in there. I don't anticipate any problem, but I've often found that fate favors the prepared."

Emrys fumbled the metal clasp on the envelope and dumped the contents onto the seat next to him. The pile strung together the story of a human Emrys Hemlock, who had been born at St. Mary's Hospital twenty-seven years ago to John and Jane Hemlock. This version of Emrys had an unused passport and a driver's license—Zackary had snapped the pictures against the apartment entrance wall the night before and texted them to Father Wilhelm—and a social security card. He was not an organ donor.

He studied his driver's license in the bursts of streetlights as the priest pulled the car onto the road. "Any chance the Order's open to feedback? Because I most certainly don't look twenty-seven."

Father Wilhelm chuckled. "It's so you can rent a car in your name without any trouble."

"I don't think you want Emrys renting *or* driving a car," Zackary chimed in.

Emrys glared at the back of Zackary's strawberry-blonde head but refrained from telling him to fuck off out of respect for their driver. He didn't give a shit about most Order members' sensibilities, but Wilhelm was alright in Emrys' book. Zackary couldn't confirm it, but he suspected that Wilhelm had been the one to shut down any attempts to heckle him or Maryam after the Peter-possession debacle, turning the microscope on Father Jonathan Claude instead. It still peeved Emrys that the Order hadn't punished that old vulture for abusing Maryam as a child, but at least Father Wilhelm had gotten him yeeted him off to Rome where he couldn't do any more damage.

Emrys dug out his wallet, slipped in the license, and stashed the other documents back in their envelope. "How old does your license say you are, Zack?"

"I actually just got mine updated," Zackary answered. "I'm back to being thirty-one now."

Emrys smirked. "So, you're a faerie cradle robber *and* a human cradle robber."

The demon glowered at him in the rearview mirror. "We're only four years apart on paper."

"That doesn't sound like a denial."

"Please excuse him, Father." Zackary flipped Emrys off, his right hand contorted between his seat and the passenger door to hide the gesture from the priest. "He doesn't exactly have what humans call 'home training.'"

"That's quite alright." Father Wilhelm chuckled as he turned on the blinker to veer onto the highway. "I haven't had this much fun shuttling folks to the airport."

By the time they reached Detroit Metropolitan Wayne County Airport, Emrys was awake enough to gape at the scale of the building and the crowds, slack-jawed and slightly starry-eyed. He found himself so distracted by the flow of cars and the blinking lights that he hardly heard Father Wilhelm's final instructions. He'd seen a lot of marvelous things in the human world but never an airport.

Judging by the stern, exhausted look on Zackary's face as they entered the ticketing terminal, he didn't share the wonder.

Emrys followed a step behind, marveling at the lines and chatter. Stopping to think about it made him realize that he'd never seen this many humans in one place before.

He'd never been under such close scrutiny in a glamour before.

He hovered a hair's breadth away from Zackary as they stood in the security line, eyeing the giant tubes with rotating arms that showed the human guards what everyone looked like on the inside. Signs warned travelers about forbidden items and the consequences of trying to bring them on board. Other travelers looked around, bored and curious, like being scrutinized and questioned by people with badges, harsh expressions, and mysterious devices decorating their belts was normal. Were some of those things weapons? How freely were they allowed to hurt people they thought were dangerous?

Emrys tried to keep his heart from racing at the idea that someone might see through his disguise by glancing his way from the corner of their eyes. What would they do if they did? What about the cameras? What if the guards separated him from Zackary and dragged him away? What if he was powerless and couldn't fight back with what little magic he knew how to use?

Or, worse, what if he summoned that deeper magic, the Hemlock magic he had never wanted and he hurt someone, and—

Zackary tapped the back of his hand. "Hey."

Emrys whirled to look at him and found a sleepy, comforting smile instead of a scowl—one that brought out the hint of crinkles around Zackary's eyes that Emrys found horrendously cute.

"It's okay." Zackary shuffled forward in line. "There's nothing to be afraid of. The Order's flown me a handful of times, and I've never had an issue."

Emrys folded his arms to fight off the desire to reach for the demon's hand. "Who said I'm afraid? I'm just a bit apprehensive." He glanced toward the nearest guard, a bored stern-looking white man clearly unhappy with being scheduled for this crack-of-dawn shift. "I'm just not used to going through situations I can't charm my way out of."

Zackary snorted and approached the counter. "I believe it."

Emrys tensed as Zackary scanned two images on his phone—boarding passes, they were called—and then showed the man a panel of his tri-fold wallet. The man leaned in, squinted, and then pointed Zackary to the end of the checkpoint where a simple baggage scanner and door-frame metal detector stood.

Emrys studied the man as he passed, scurrying after Zackary as he asked, "What did you—"

Zackary softly shushed him and shook his head. "Wait 'till we're through."

Emrys closed his mouth and willingly did what he was told for once, stripping off his shoes and jacket and patting down his pockets before stepping through the metal detector. Once on the other side and again fully dressed, he massaged his aching neck as he waited for Zackary to tie his shoes. Had he really been that tense the entire time?

Zackary slung on his own backpack and patted Emrys on the shoulder as if they were teammates who had just finished practice. "C'mon. I'll get you a coffee to celebrate your first TSA crossing."

Emrys hustled to catch up. "But what just happened?"

Zackary pulled out his wallet and passed it to Emrys. Inside, across from Zackary's license, was a slip of paper with three lines of Latin. His mother had claimed to know some Latin from her own mother, whose father had been a Roman mortal, according to family legend but she hadn't taught Emrys before her death—not that he'd been interested.

"Long story short, the Order has tendrils everywhere," Zackary explained as they walked. "Father Wilhelm called ahead to whatever connections he has to make sure one of our people was working security."

"That...is..." Emrys tried to find the right words as he handed back the wallet. "That is a bit terrifying, honestly."

"Oh, absolutely." Zackary slipped his wallet into his jeans. "Reason five hundred and eleven why I never want to find myself on their bad side."

Emrys blinked. "How long is this list, exactly?"

Zackary gave a wry smile. "Not sure. It gets longer every day."

Zackary made good on his promise of coffee, which Emrys made sure to order with extra espresso. Even with the long line and the small staff, they arrived with an hour to spare, much to Emrys' annoyance. Once settled in a stiff, pleather seat, he pulled out his phone and navigated to the reading application, where he found the stupid high school vampire book Maryam had badgered him into reading. Three pages in, Emrys realized someone was staring at him. He looked up to find a baby, no more than a few months old, peeking over their mother's shoulder, wide eyes glued on Emrys as they gummed their blanket. Emrys smiled and waved, securing the infant's attention. He covered his eyes, then peeked over his fingers. The infant squealed and thrashed, unable to contain the amusement in their tiny body, making Emrys laugh.

Zackary looked up from his book at the sound, glancing from his travel companion to the baby, then back with a slightly amused grin. "Didn't take you for a kid person."

Emrys shrugged. "I like kids well enough. Best not to let me around the ones who can talk, though. I'm a bad influence. Hard to damage babies, provided you keep them safe and you're gentle with them." He played another round of peek-a-boo, getting another giggle from the baby and finding himself smiling wider than he had in awhile. He turned to find Zachary grinning, too, his expression now bemused. Emrys dropped his smile and scowled.

Zackary blinked, his grin faltering. "What?"

"You're mocking me."

"I am not." Zackary rolled his eyes and settled back against his seat. "I've just never seen you like this before, is all."

"Like what?"

The demon studied Emrys for a moment, his green eyes seeming to look past Emrys' glamour, past his quips and attitude. "Truly joyful."

Heat rose in Emrys' cheeks. The demon seemed to like what he saw, but Emrys didn't know what to do with that—the idea that someone liked something about him beyond what he let them see.

He leaned back in his chair, ankle over his knee, and returned to his phone. "I don't know what you're talking about. I'm always joyful."

Zackary scoffed against the plastic lid of his coffee. "You're always *flirty*. And pleasant, when you're not being a pain in the ass. Those aren't the same thing as joyful."

Emrys shrugged, not looking to give any more of himself than what had already slipped out.

"Do you think you'd ever want to be a dad?" Zackary asked after a quiet moment.

Emrys cackled, doing his best to rein in the reaction out of respect for other passengers. He stopped short when he saw the frown on Zackary's face. "Oh, you were serious?"

"Of course, I'm serious. Who asks something like that as a joke?"

Emrys let out a dismissive *pfff* before laughing again. "Someone who knows me, for starters." He looked back to Zackary, expecting him to shake his head or roll his eyes—something to signal that he dismissed Emrys' answer as childish and unworthy of follow-up. Instead, Emrys found those green eyes still boring into him, looking for more than he had any right to.

Emrys played with the drawstrings of his hoodie, slouching in his seat to make himself smaller. "I'm not...good, Zack. I'm feral, selfish, and shallow. No one like that has any business bringing a child into this world. They're just going to grow up to be a monster. Hell, I had a wonderful mother and look how I turned out."

"That's not fair. Your mother was taken from you."

Emrys shrugged. "I was a bastard running wild in the Hemlock court's shadows. I would have turned out wrong no matter who raised me. Besides, any child of mine born with my horns would have a target on their back the second they came out of the womb." He brushed his hair with his hand, motioning to where the ram horns curled around his pointed ears when his glamour was down. "I'm not doing that to another person."

Emrys watched Zackary watching him, hating the pity he saw. He didn't need it. Didn't want it. He'd made peace with what and who he was, and he didn't need some judgmental Abrahamic bastard to make him feel bad about any of it, no matter how hot he was.

He turned back to his phone. "Why? You trying to trap me with a kid or something?"

Zackary laughed at that, the heaviness of the moment gone. "I'm not sure that's physically possible."

Emrys smirked. "Please. Have you seen me? I'm extremely bree-da—"

"Don't." Zackary's breath brushed Emrys' ear as he grabbed his arm and leaned in, hissing the warning. "Don't you dare finish that sentence. We are in public."

The authority beneath Zackary's words sent a bolt of heat through Emrys' body, tangling his stomach and sent his heart racing. Finally. Fucking finally, Emrys had gotten under Zackary's skin and dragged him out to play. A smirk came to his lips as he turned to face Zackary, his mouth practically brushing the demon's as he whispered back, "What are you going to do about it if I do?"

A dark fire flashed in Zackary's eyes. It was brief, a glimmer of hunger before he slipped back behind his civilized mask, but Emrys knew he'd caught it. His breath hitched, and his jacket and hoodie suddenly felt too tight. Had it always been this hot in here?

Zackary's grip loosened on Emrys' arm. "I'm not going to do anything because a reaction is exactly what you want." He pulled away, muttering "Brat" under his breath. Because of course he had to have the final word.

Emrys had been called a brat plenty of times before. With him being, well, *him*, it was par for the course, but something about that word on Zackary's tongue had him wishing he could get on his knees right there in the terminal—he could show that prude of a demon just how much of a brat he could really be, show him how good it felt to just take what he wanted for once.

Fuck, how amazing would it feel to give him everything?

Emrys blinked, shocked at himself. This wasn't how this went. This wasn't how any of this went. Emrys held the reins. Always. Even when he was being pinned down and fucked out of his mind. He wasn't supposed to truly give any of himself to the other person. That wasn't allowed. Not anymore.

He got to his feet, walking off without any real direction.

"Where are you going?" Zackary called after him.

Emrys caught a glimpse of a restroom sign. "Bathroom."

Once inside, he splashed cold water on his face and breathed deep behind his hands until the heat beneath his skin melted away. This was stupid. How many times had he implied, or outright said, that he was ready to do just about anything with Zackary at a moment's notice?

But "ready" and "wanting" were two different things to him. "Ready" meant he was down to chase an orgasm. It meant he was playing to win, that the other person was the one giving in. "Wanting" meant...he didn't know, but he knew in his gut it was different. Dangerous.

Emrys looked at himself in the mirror over his wet hands, shook his head, then reached for the paper towel dispenser. This was nonsense. Emrys just hadn't gotten laid recently, thanks to Zackary holding out, trying to be a "gentleman" or whatever.

Maybe he needed to cut his losses and leave before this became a problem. His living arrangement would be as good as over the second he gave into Zackary's silly proposals for dates and romance anyhow, because things like that didn't last. Not for him.

The thought of leaving made him pause, but he immediately shook it away. He'd at least finish this mission with Zackary, then see how he felt. Emrys was a lot of things, most of them horrible and whorish, but he wasn't so terrible that he would abandon someone who had opened his home and family to him just because he spooked himself with his own ridiculous thoughts. He had to believe he was better than that.

By the time he left the restroom, the other passengers had began to cluster around the terminal, only vaguely aware of what it meant to form a line. He joined Zackary toward the back of the formation, only to discover a much bigger issue at the sight of just how small the airplane was.

This...this was going to be a problem.

Emrys hadn't ever stopped to wonder if he might be claustrophobic. Between his short height, slight frame, and magic, there were few tight spots he couldn't wiggle his way out of, but escaping the plane would result in a plummet to the ground a million miles below, magic or no.

Zackary stopped at the second to last row, then turned to Emrys. "Did you want the window seat? You've never seen a plane take off before."

"That's very kind." Emrys slipped off his backpack. "But hell no."

Zackary laughed, then stopped short as he studied Emrys' face. "Are you alright?"

"I'll be fine." Sliding into his seat, he muttered, "Once I get off this damn death trap of a contraption."

"I could ask a steward to bring you water or something." Zackary fought to shove his bag under the seat in front of him.

Emrys fastened his belt and sat with his arms crossed, one knee bouncing. "Really, it's fine. I don't want to make a fuss."

"Really? *You* don't want to make a fuss?"

Emrys glared in response.

The plane seemed to shrink in on itself the more packed it grew until Emrys thought he might fold in on himself. He didn't hear a word the steward said during the safety demonstration—he was too busy keeping his breaths even and slow while his mind raced through a million questions.

Why the hell had he agreed to this? Why hadn't he cut and run right there in the airport? Did he really think he could do anything good for a change, even if the siren wasn't...*her*? He'd been useless to stop bad things from happening then, just like with his mother, just like now if this plane went down, trapping them all inside. All the magic in the world couldn't possibly keep this thing in the air. They'd all die, and he'd die as uselessly as he'd lived. Wait, were his charms working? Why could he smell the iron of the plane? What if they gave out and the iron poisoned him, smothering him to death in this horrible thing where he couldn't get out—

Something below the plane gave a loud *bang*, and Emrys yelped. He caught the startled looks of the humans around him and dropped his head in his hands to hide his burning face. Fuck, this was...embarrassing? Emrys couldn't remember the last time he was embarrassed.

Embarrassed and wanting. In the same day. He wondered if this was what one of the lighter layers of Hell was like.

"Hey." Zackary's hand gently slipped into Emrys', his face close and his voice low. "Tell me what's wrong."

"I just..." Emrys winced at another mechanical sound. "I don't like relying on this *thing*." Emrys gestured around them to the plane. "It's cramped and made of iron. What if something goes wrong? We're trapped."

Zackary squeezed his hand and came a bit closer. "If something goes wrong, I've got you. I won't let anything happen to you."

"You can't promise that."

"No, but you've got to trust that I'd fight like hell to keep my word."

Emrys studied Zackary, realizing just how close he was—those sharp green eyes and that smirk Emrys was convinced he wasn't aware of—the one that revealed that the soft-spoken, humble, level-headed Zackary Bishop could get just a little bit cocky sometimes.

He was so very good. So very worth truly wanting.

The plane lurched. Emrys squeezed his eyes shut as he sank further into his seat. Could he just die now? Was that an option?

Zackary interlaced their fingers and sat back. "Look—these seats have movies and stuff on them." He tapped the black screen in the headrest in front of them. It came alive, displaying a handful of recent releases and a menu at the side. A steward walked by, double-checking seatbelts and offering packets of headphones. Zackary took a pair with a polite smile, unwrapped them, and slipped the jack into the bottom of the screen before handing one earbud to Emrys. "It's not a super long flight, but it might distract you."

His only response was a blink at first. He couldn't string together a thought right now. "Why...why don't you pick?" He gingerly swiped across the screen, making the choices move. "I don't recognize most of this."

Zackary motioned to an animated film, a big, beaming smile on his stupid, wantable face. "I haven't seen this one in forever. Maryam used to play it on repeat for *hours* when she was little. I never thought I'd actually want to see it again."

"That's fine."

Zackary selected the film and sat back in his seat, still holding Emrys' hand. Thanks to the feeling of skin touching skin, Emrys hardly noticed the film or the lift of the plane.

It was the most innocent form of contact he'd had in ages, and it consumed every bit of him, like their little spat at the terminal, but in a way that soothed Emrys like chamomile and lavender rather than set his blood racing.

"I think I'm better now," he said as the cabin lights went low. "You don't have to keep holding my hand."

"It's okay. I don't mind." Zackary gave Emrys' hand a playful squeeze. "So long as you act right for once."

Emrys' heart hammered so hard that he didn't have any space left in his head to form a quip. He only nodded and settled into his seat.

Sleep took him moments later, leaving him with the thought of how incredibly fucked he was.

Zackary Bishop's feelings for Emrys Hemlock were changing. Morphing. And that was a big fucking problem. He'd braced himself for Emrys' usual Emrys-ness: the teasing, flirting, raunchy suggestions, and smart-ass remarks—but then that damn pixie had made him feel so many different things in the span of thirty minutes that Zackary had nearly gotten whiplash.

The smile on Emrys' face as he played with that baby had lit something up in Zackary akin to awe and excitement. He'd never seen Emrys' face so bright before, so unabashedly present and joyful. With a ping of dread, Zackary realized that Emrys wasn't only attractive. He was genuinely beautiful.

Then Emrys said all those harsh, cruel things about himself, twisting Zackary up inside with the desperate urge to tell him that he was wrong, that he was none of those things. And then, on the heels of those comments, he'd gone back to his old bullshit—challenging

Zackary. Taunting him. Teasing him. Inviting him to embrace the most carnal version of himself—the version he'd rip out and burn if he could.

No sooner had Zackary locked that fire away did Emrys have a full-blown panic attack, pulling Zackary into protector mode. Despite how clearly Emrys had stated he was only interested in sex, Zackary couldn't shake the growing need to protect him—to shield him from a world that had been so cruel it seeped into him, under his skin and into his blood, until he began devouring himself like a cancer.

Zackary dropped his gaze to their clasped hands and gently stroked his thumb against Emrys' cool skin—faeries always ran cool, for some reason—and silently cursed himself like the broody old gargoyle Emrys said he was. What the hell was wrong with him? He'd been in this standoff with Emrys for months, with no sign of the pixie wavering. It had been fun for a while, watching Emrys cringe and wriggle every time Zackary met his raunchy suggestions with sweetness, but Zackary would be lying if he said it wasn't starting to hurt a bit, watching Emrys fail to realize, or blatantly ignore, how much Zackary wanted to give him.

So, why couldn't Zackary put an end to it?

The plane lurched as it hit the ground, jolting the pixie awake. He blinked away the sleep as he stretched, nearly knocking Zackary in the face. Oh, look," he said through a yawn. We're not dead."

Zackary gave a tired smile as he gathered his things as best he could. Did you sleep at all last night?"

Yes, but I'm a delicate flower of a thing." Emrys massaged the back of his neck with a pained, scrunched expression. My rhythm has been disturbed and now I'm wilting."

Zackary rolled his eyes.

Once off the plane, he navigated the two of them through the small airport and out the door, having to snatch Emrys by the collar when he attempted to retreat inside at the first blast of breath-stealing icy air. He ignored Emrys' claim that he would sooner brave a plane again before staying in such cold, dragging him to a bench where they waited for a shuttle to the car rental kiosk.

The second the two were in the vehicle, Emrys cranked the heat and the seat warmers, burrowing into the puffy coat he'd dug from his backpack, arms pulled in, and legs up against his chest.

How in the holy hell does anyone live up here willingly?" Emrys asked through chattering teeth.

Zackary chuckled to himself as he navigated the car to the gate. I thought you said you'd been up here before."

In the *summer*. Like a *sane* person. Do I strike you as someone keen on freezing to death?"

Emrys had seemed keen on equally asinine things in the past, so Zackary didn't bother answering.

The rising sun bathed the stretches of surrounding grasslands and woods in icy gray light, muting any hint of color in the landscape. Winter in Detroit could be a harsh, violent, dangerous thing. Winter here carried a stillness that boarded on eerie. At least, today it did. Zackary doubted a place could amass snow this high without its share of intense weather.

Did you ever watch *The Tommyknockers*?" Zackary asked. It was based on a Stephen King book. This plane full of people ends up back in time, and the past is completely empty. This sort of looks like that."

Emrys began to crawl out of his coat. Can't say I have." He stretched his legs and propped his head with a fist as he leaned against the car door. I'm not terribly keen on cinema, especially horror."

Zackary smirked, though his gaze stayed on the wet road. Horror movies provide quite a few opportunities to hold hands if you get scared."

Emrys sat up a tad taller. Zackary Bishop, are you *flirting* with me?"

Damn it, he was. Again. After just chastising himself for not letting this go.

I suppose I am." Zackary slowed the car to a stop as the road ended at a stretch of highway, checked the GPS in the console, and clicked the turn signal to the right. "Romantically."

Emrys snorted. Disgusting."

Oh, come on." Zackary chuckled as he pulled out onto the highway. You've never enjoyed a bit of emotional investment with your sexcapades?" It was a genuine question. Regardless of their little game, they had an hour on the road—might as well fill it with a real conversation.

Once. Horrible mistake." Emrys began fiddling with the radio. "Why are you so fixated on it?"

Zackary thought for a moment, wondering if his attempts to reach Emrys were failing because a game wasn't what they needed—what they needed was honesty. "There's a certain quiet strength in shared vulnerability, I think," he said. "A fortitude, if you will, that comes when you have a safe place to lay down your burdens and build a space to heal, if only for a time, from the things that others have done to us."

Zackary spared Emrys a glance to ensure he was still listening. He had gone still. Not just quiet. *Still*. Zackary could see him from his peripherals, staring with an open expression on his face almost akin to contemplation. Deep thought, even.

As soon as it registered, it was gone and Emrys turned his focus back to the bleak gray landscape. Sounds like a lot of work. Maybe stick to normal stuff like bondage."

Zackary scoffed. Your bondage clearly isn't intricate enough if you think emotional connection is easier."

Emrys whirled around with a sharp squeak of shock, his mouth hanging open. *Zackary Bishop.* Are you admitting to being *kinky?*"

Don't get greedy." The demon smirked. Start sharing a few of your secrets and maybe you'll get a few more of mine."

Emrys pouted. You tease."

I'm literally just asking you to let me get to know you better."

Like I said." Emrys turned back to the window. You're a tease. Enticing me with the possibility of getting tied up only to ask me about my feelings."

Zackary sighed and switched the radio station, doing his best to ignore the little pang of disappointment in his gut.

Thirty minutes down the road, the forest gave way to the pale vastness of Lake Superior stretching out to the horizon. Emrys gasped. Despite needing to keep his eyes on the road, Zackary agreed with the sentiment. It seemed impossible that something so vast, so endless could be contained on all sides—a minor, volatile goddess that would not be denied her recognition despite her frame of shores and freshwater frozen below the surface. Each twist and turn in the road revealed a new curve along the shore that showcased a new span of ice and water. Circlets of ice bobbed on lazy waves and bumped into one another. Along another stretch of snowy beach, a smooth plane of ice stretched out into eternity. Around another corner, snow piled high and peaked like meringue. In a small harbor carved out of the sandstone cliff, shards of ice jutted into the air like a pit of needles.

Zackary marveled in the small moments he could spend staring out at the water. It didn't matter how massive, tall, or powerful the things humans built could be—they could never compare to the world they had been given.

Zackary spared Emrys a glance. Any other potential killers come to mind?"

Emrys' gaze darted between the birch trees that lined the road. I think Father Wilhelm was right, unfortunately." He sat back in his seat, his mood significantly deflated. Seems like an ideal place for a siren to hunt. Thin ice, sharp drops most people can't climb, water so cold you can't breathe—they would love this place."

I can't decide if that's comforting or not."

Nor can I." Emrys turned his attention to his phone. Best to err on the side of 'not.'"

Zackary nearly missed the carved Welcome to Glace" sign, thanks to the mountain of dirty snow that buried it.

The town spread out before them to the north, thinning against the beach to a small sandy harbor framed by rocky cliffs on one side and a stone pier topped with a lighthouse on the other. The southern half melted into the winter woods with small square houses providing pops of color against the gray, barren landscape. Emrys sat up straight to marvel at the quaint downtown. Red wire hearts and pink metallic garlands scaled the streetlights while paper cut-out cupids smiled from storefronts.

Emrys smirked at Zackary over his shoulder. We still never settled on Valentine's plans."

Yes, we did." Zackary checked the GPS as it led them out of the other side of town. We're working."

Emrys gave a dismissive click of his tongue and turned back to his window. I mean...the door in your office *does* lock."

Zackary pressed the button to open Emrys' window, blasting him with freezing air. Emrys gave a small shriek before managing to roll it back up.

Ten minutes past Glace, the scenery morphed into barren fields reserved for crops, though what was expected to grow in such a cool climate was beyond Zackary. Within one of the fields sat a tall, slender farmhouse, worn and faded with age, but with clean windows alight with a warm glow. Zackary pulled into the snow-packed driveway and parked alongside the house. The front door flew open with a bang as he turned off the car, unleashing a pair of lanky black labs across the yard.

A petite woman emerged from the house, most of her height made of a thick frizzy white ponytail on top of her head. Zeus! Odin! Manners!"

Neither dog heeded, both greeting Zackary by jumping up and knocking him back against the car. He laughed, scratching the back of both dogs' heads as they sniffed and nipped at his arms. Their owner joined Zackary in the driveway, yanking both dogs down by the scruff of their necks, displaying more strength than he expected from someone so petite.

Damn knuckleheads." She smiled up at Zackary, still crouched to control the dogs. There was something familiar about her face—something about the crooked curve of her mouth and the light in her green eyes that Zackary had seen before but couldn't quite place. I'm sorry. No matter what I do, these two are absolute nightmares when I have company." She released one dog to offer him her hand. I'm Gracie. I'm an old friend of the Order."

Zackary shook her hand, careful not to squeeze Gracie's papery, bony fingers too hard. Zackary Bishop. Call me Zack."

Lovely to meet you, Zack." Gracie snatched the free dog before he could run for the other side of the car. Father Wilhelm said there would be two of you?"

Here." Emrys waved over the hood of the car as he got out, slinging his backpack over his shoulder. Walking around the car, he offered Gracie his hand with a winning smile. Emrys Hemlock, ma'am."

No need to be so formal." Gracie fought to wrangle her dogs, making Emrys flinch back. Knock it off!" The dogs shrank back at her tone. I'm sorry, Emrys."

He gave her a sheepish smile. It's fine. It's their house, after all."

Gracie grabbed a long, gnawed stick from the ground and threw it out into the field. Get after it, you monsters."

The dogs bolted through the snow, barreling over each other in the chase. Zackary noted the way Emrys' shoulders relaxed.

C'mon." Gracie motioned toward the house. Let's get your boys warmed up before sending you out into town."

Zackary grabbed his bag from the backseat and walked alongside Emrys toward the rickety porch. I didn't know you were afraid of big dogs."

I'm not afraid," Emrys hissed. They're just too unpredictable for my liking."

Like how you're 'not afraid' of airplanes?"

Emrys flashed Zackary a withering look and the demon tried not to laugh.

It's alright to be afraid of things, Em."

As Emrys followed Zackary through the door, he muttered, Not where I'm from."

Inside, the two found a living room untouched by the last three or four decades of changing fashions. Faded corduroy furniture sat atop beige carpet while striped wallpaper framed gilded, touch-activated lamps. Zackary spied a quaint kitchen through one wooden archway while another led to a well-stocked study.

Can I get you boys some coffee? Tea?"

Whichever is more convenient for you," Zackary said.

Same for me," Emrys added.

Gracie disappeared into the kitchen, leaving the two to study the photos on the wall. Past versions of Gracie smiled out from all over the world, Machu Picchu, the Taj Mahal, the Sahara, the Vatican, and Tokyo, like a spread-out flip book of the woman's life. Zackary scanned the pictures, watching in real-time as the woman aged—her vibrant red hair fading to stark white and the years wearing against her skin, but that bright smile never faltered and the light never dimmed in her green eyes. Atop the mantle sat a faded, grainy image featuring a particularly young smiling Gracie and a scowling man that Zackary had the misfortune of knowing anywhere. The surprise made him do a double take. He crossed the room to examine it, not quite believing what he saw.

Sure enough, a young Gracie beamed at the camera while Father Jonathan Claude scowled, his face significantly less creased from years of frowning and his head covered in meticulously styled thick blonde hair, but it was still him alright.

"Gracie, you know Father Claude?" Zackary called, gaze glued to the photograph. Who did she look like? He knew her younger face even better than her current one.

Gracie joined him and Emrys in the living room with an ornate coffee percolator in one hand and a tray with mugs, cream, and sugar balanced in the other. "You mean Jon?" She gave a tired smile as she set the coffee and the tray on a table. "I did, once. We would have been in the same graduating class at the Rosary Order's Academy of Exorcism." She placed her hands on her hips and studied the picture from beside the coffee table and sighed. "But life put us on different paths." She poured a cup of coffee and handed it to Emrys, who took it with a small "Thank you."

Zackary turned back to the photograph to study it one more time. A knot in his gut told him to leave it alone, not to dig where he had no business digging in the home of a woman he didn't know, but there was something in the openness of young Gracie's smile...the point of her nose and the curve of her eyebrows...and then there was the stern line of Claude's mouth and the way he parted his blonde hair all those years ago...

Zackary could only blink as the world fell out from under him.

Emrys cleared his throat, startling Zackary back into the living room. "This coffee is immaculate, Gracie. Where did you get it?"

"A roaster I befriended years ago when I was in Rome." Gracie poured herself a cup and sat back in her plush olive-green armchair. "I can't drink espresso like I used to. I was so pleased when I saw he was branching out to do American-style brews."

Zackary joined the two and dropped down on the sofa. "Sorry. Didn't mean to get so distracted." He helped himself to a shortbread cookie. "It's just crazy to see him as a young man. I thought maybe he was born old and bitter."

Gracie chuckled over her mug. "You wouldn't be the first person to say that, and I doubt you'll be the last." She took a sip. "Enough about him, though. We have murders to solve." She sat up a bit taller in her chair. "What do you know about the case?"

"Father Wilhelm gave us a pretty thick file on the details." Zackary helped himself to coffee. "Did you know the victims?"

Gracie frowned. "Not well. They attended the local high school back when I taught, but I never had either of them in class. They seemed like sweet boys. Their coven is taking the situation so hard."

Emrys ticked up an eyebrow. "The file didn't mention that they were part of the coven. The only mention of the coven at all was Father Wilhelm's worry that they'd be targeted."

"Not surprising. Don't let all the snow fool you. This town has roots as deep, twisted, and Evangelical as anywhere down south. We're a town of something like seven hundred people with six churches and talk of another on the way. When a metaphysical store opened up here in town a few years ago, it nearly caused a riot. Every once and a while, people get it in their brains that maybe they can get it shut down on the myth that it's peddling Satanism to kids or some other bullshit scare tactic." Gracie made a startled noise and covered her mouth with her hand. "I'm sorry."

Zackary smiled. "I run a bar when I'm not chasing demons. We've both heard plenty worse." He took a long sip of his coffee. Damn, Emrys was right. It *was* immaculate. He added a bit of cream and sugar to bring out the notes of vanilla.

Emrys took a cookie from the tray and dipped it in his mug. "How'd you end up in a town like this?" He motioned to the pictures on the wall with the dunked cookie, then popped it in his mouth. "Doesn't seem like your kind of place after all the things you've seen—both natural and supernatural."

Gracie sighed, her shoulders drooping. "I needed quiet after all that. I had things I needed to think about, so when I retired, I took a job teaching English here. My parents were originally from Marquette, so I guess a part of me thought I was coming home to rest, in a way." She studied her drink for a quiet moment. "There's not a place in this world remote enough to hide from yourself, boys. Don't forget that."

Zackary worried it might be impolite to remind Gracie that he and Emrys were both definitely older than her, so he said nothing and drank his coffee.

Gracie snapped back to herself with a smile. "I told the coven you were coming. Said you could help stop this from happening again." She checked her watch. "I told them you'd meet them at the only pizza place in town. Figured that would draw a tad less suspicion than the shop."

"Thank you for assisting us so much," Zackary said. "It's very kind of you."

Gracie waved away the comment. "No thanks needed. Whatever is doing this is a bully, plain and simple, and I can't stand bullies."

Zackary finished his coffee instead of informing Gracie what a bully her old friend, Father Jonathan Claude, had turned out to be.

With their refreshments finished, Gracie showed the two where they'd be staying—a pair of small bedrooms on the second story. Both contained a single twin-sized bed on an old metal frame with a patchwork quilt, a dresser, a closet, and a small writing desk. They hadn't been used since Gracie stopped taking foster kids a few years ago. She had moved her room to the first floor to avoid the risk of falling, leaving the boys with plenty of privacy. Zackary flashed Emrys a sharp glare to keep the pixie's mouth shut about the third room, which included a queen-sized bed. For once, Emrys seemed to listen.

With their bags dropped off and the address for the one pizza place in town written on a sticky note, the two headed back out to the car. Gracie would not be coming with them—she had work to attend to out in the shed. Zackary played with Odin and Zeus so Emrys could get into the car un-harassed, then joined him, patting off snow and dirt from his short game of fetch.

"What held your attention so tightly when you found that picture of Claude?" Emrys asked, burrowing back against his heated seat.

Zackary turned on the car and punched the address in the GPS. "It was just unexpected. That's all."

Emrys snorted. "Liar. The look on your face said you were calculating. A lot."

Zackary silently pulled the car out of the driveway and onto the road as he tried to decide what to say. Even if he was right in his suspicions—which he couldn't be, because they were preposterous—they weren't his to share, especially not with Emrys. "It doesn't matter," he finally said. "Besides, we have locals to meet."

The savory smells of baking bread, cheese, and meat made Emrys' stomach growl, reminding him that they hadn't eaten since three in the morning, leaving him to wonder if they would have time for lunch here. Under different circumstances, he might have actually liked the place—the old-fashioned stained-glass lamps over the tables, the bare brickwork of the walls, the hanging pictures laying out the building's past. The place was cozy and, more importantly, warm.

A teenager with a braces-lined grin approached them from the checkout counter. "Can I get you a table?"

Motion in the distance nabbed Emrys' attention. He looked toward the back to find a slender wisp of a woman waving them down from the farthest booth, her small frame nearly swallowed whole by her oversized hoodie. Two others on either side of her watched Zackary and Emrys wearily.

"I believe we see our party," Zackary said with his customer service smile. "I will take water with lemon when you get a moment, though."

Emrys followed a step behind, unsure what to think or how to conduct himself. His mother had told him stories of witches in the Old World—mortals, mostly women, from all social stations and faiths, who would join the goodfolk for reveries or leave out bread and honey in exchange for little favors and blessings. Some even ran away to live forever in Faerieland as musicians and lovers. When goodfolk stole away to the New World, whether because human expansion was driving them out or purely out of curiosity, they found fewer witches joined them. Too many of those humans served the three gods from the rocky hills of Palaestina—the gods who had swallowed the indigenous spirits of Europe whole, along with their peoples' tongues and cultures, with their talk of a Son who offered salvation from his violent, vengeful Father—the same Father who had damned Zackary for daring to enjoy, to feel, anything outside of blind devotion to Him—and a mysterious spirit who was sometimes a Spirit and sometimes a Ghost. Those gods seemed to hate everything that was not cold and cruel and made of suffering. The humans who stole this New World were determined to rebuild the land in Their image.

Witches did come, though, hiding the old ways sewn in the hems of dresses and tonics that cured fevers and coughs. As the Europeans moved west, witches sometimes followed, joining goodfolk who had settled in the endless woods, especially in the mountains of Appalachia—mountains carved from the same ancient stones as home. Even there, their numbers dwindled.

Emrys heard that some were adopting the old ways as more and more people abandoned the Three Gods, but they had not learned like they had in the old days. They learned from books written by strangers, internet forums, and friends. Emrys didn't know what to make of witches like that.

These witches seemed alright as far as mortals went. The slender one, the one who had flagged them down, had sharp, calculating eyes that Emrys instantly liked—they were like his but serious. The girl on her left, short and curvy, her face framed in blonde curls, seemed less sure of herself. Her round blue eyes took Emrys and Zackary in like they might be wolves in men's clothing. (Or women's. Emrys had stolen this particular sweater from Maryam's closet.) On the right sat a boy who looked like he might launch himself across the table at Zackary and Emrys if they so much as looked at the girls wrong, given the murderous glint in his dark eyes.

"Are you the men Miss Gracie called about Collin and Ian?" the center girl asked, her voice a deeper, richer honey alto than Emrys was expecting. He liked the confidence and calculation in it.

"That's right." Zackary took a business card from his wallet and handed it to her. The other two gathered around. "I'm Zackary Bishop. This is my partner, Emrys Hemlock. We work for the Rosary Order, specializing in supernatural disturbances."

The center girl snorted. "I'd say what happened to our friends was more than a disturbance."

Zackary's smile twitched. "Just trying to be delicate. I was told you were all close."

The blonde girl nodded and squeezed the other girl's hand. "Ian was my cousin. Second cousin, technically, but still." She crumpled and rolled a napkin in her other hand. "We grew up together."

The boy's expression grew harsher. "Collin was my foster brother for a while. Back when my mom couldn't keep me. His parents are nuts, but he was a good dude."

Emrys' chest tightened as his soul fell through the floor with despair. Judging by the look on Zackary's face, he felt the same. His shoulders fell, his expression creased, and his gaze darted from one young face to another in a failed attempt to find the right words.

"'Sorry' doesn't even begin to convey how my heart breaks for you all." Zackary eased off his coat, slow and careful, like he might spook the three witches like deer. "May we sit?"

The center woman motioned to the booth. The group adjusted, closing in closer to one another while Emrys and Zackary each took a side of the curved booth. Zackary took out a pen and small leather notebook that had seen better days—the cover fraying and faded, streaked with stray pen markings, and the pages poofed up from spills, dog ears, and general use. Emrys could hardly believe there were even any pages left. Part of him worried he just might run out and have to write on a napkin to finish the conversation.

"Let's start with the basics—I read a lot of names in the files, so I'd like to put some faces to them."

The two on the outside glanced at the center woman to speak first. She gave them weary looks, then sighed. "My name's Jupiter Adams."

The other girl spoke next. "Samantha Westra. Everyone calls me Sammy."

"I'm Stone," said the boy.

Zackary and Emrys waited for a last name. When it didn't come, Zackary prompted, "Stone...what?"

Stone glared. "Why? You're not a cop."

Emrys choked on a laugh. Both girls groaned—Sammy rolling her eyes, muttering "Stoney, come on, man," while Jupiter massaged her temple.

Zackary just scribbled in the notebook. "Jupiter Adams...Sammy Westra...Stone Why-You're-Not-A-Cop. Got it."

Jupiter snorted, Sammy gave Zackary a grateful smile, and Stone's glare sharpened.

Zackary looked back at them. "Outside of family relations, how did you start hanging out?"

Jupiter shrugged. "We met at school. We were all into weird stuff. The three of us, anyway." She motioned to Sammy and Stone. "Collins and Ian didn't start hanging out with us until this last fall."

"Can you expand on what you mean by 'weird stuff'?"

The trio seemed to have an entire conversation with their expressions. Sammy appeared uncertain again. Stone gave both of the girls dark, warning looks, and Jupiter went back to doing calculations as she watched the outsiders.

Again, Jupiter spoke for the group. "We each found our way to magic and the gods on our own, then found each other when kids started teasing us for it. It turned out we were all queer, too, so we took care of each other." Jupiter glanced around the restaurant. "This town isn't exactly safe for people like us." She gave a dry smirk. "They can tolerate weirdos until they start taking estrogen and wearing dresses, apparently." She went quiet as the waitress came by with Zackary's water and a pair of menus.

Emrys noticed the way the teenager eyed the witches nervously.

When the girl was out of earshot, Jupiter spoke again. "My little sister used to play soccer with her." She stabbed at the ice in her own cup, brow furrowed and mouth downturned. "When they'd do sleepovers, she'd be the first to ask me for a tarot reading. Now she pretends like she doesn't know me."

Sammy wrung a paper napkin until it frayed. "She used to ask me for her horoscope when she was having boy trouble."

Emrys' brow pulled together. "You said Collin and Ian only started hanging out with you this autumn. Why?"

Stone's dark gaze darted around the restaurant. "You guys *sure* you're not cops?"

Emrys snorted. "You want us to cross our hearts or something?"

Zackary flashed him a dirty look, but Stone gave a satisfied huff of breath and smirked.

Jupiter elbowed him. "Stone, don't."

He rolled his eyes. "You're the one who said we can trust them since Miss Gracie trusts them."

"We don't know if the boys were even right," Sammy added.

Stone scoffed. "They wouldn't lie about something like that. Especially not Ian."

Zackary frowned. "Lie about what?"

Stone's gaze darted between Zackary and Emrys. "Ian was bi. Collin was gay. They came out to us after hanging around a few weeks back in September. The first week in October, they put feelers out to see if their parents would be safe to come out to, despite Collin's dad being the pastor at the biggest church in town and Ian's dad being the youth leader at the same church. They both learned they'd be kicked out."

Emrys flinched as if the words were a blow. Across the table, Zackary dropped his gaze to the table, body language taut as he began taking notes. Sammy took Jupiter's hand and squeezed.

Stone sat back against the booth, hands cradling his right knee as he crossed his legs. "November comes around, and Collin finds his dad making out with the church pianist during the Thanksgiving potluck, who happens to be Ian's aunt. Collin goes to Ian's dad, not wanting to break his mom's heart right out of the gate. The bastard tells him to shut up about it. That no one will believe him. Conveniently, his aunt takes a new job down in St. Ignace two weeks later."

Zackary took a break from writing to ask, "Did Collin tell his mother?"

Stone scoffed. "Sure did. She just got real quiet and told Collin to stop telling lies about his father."

Emrys could only blink in reaction to that. Zackary stopped writing for a moment, eyes still glued to his notebook as if he were trying to process what he had just written. He cleared his throat and sat up. "So, a pair of closeted teenagers from prominent families in the same church learn that their families are intertwined in an affair. The most important adults in their lives either help cover it up or don't believe them. How do we go from that to them being dead and you three somehow being whispered about?"

Stone opened his mouth to answer. Emrys raised a hand to stop him. "We're asking in an 'agents investigating the supernatural' way. Not in a cop way."

The witches had another silent conversation.

Jupiter leaned forward, her hands folded on the table, eyes steely and unblinking. "I need you two to understand that the spell the boys asked us to perform was never supposed to kill anyone. Not their dads, not Ian's aunt, and definitely not them. They lost all faith in the God their families had spent their whole lives preaching about—the God who apparently commanded their parents to kick them out for being queer. They felt powerless. Hell, in a lot of ways, they *were* powerless."

Emrys nodded. "So, they turned to you and the Old Gods."

"Exactly." Jupiter dropped her gaze, and her voice grew soft. "But we didn't understand the spell." She raised one hand to massage her temple. "Not the way we thought we did."

A chill shot down Emrys' spine like ice as the pieces fell into place. "You didn't read the spell before you performed it?"

Sammy jumped to Jupiter's defense. "We translated what we could. *Multiple* times. It didn't all make sense, but none of it talked about death. It sounded more like the people involved wouldn't be able to perform sexually until the curse was lifted."

Emrys did his best to swallow down his rising anger. Of course, they hadn't ensured they completely understood the spell—that would require a level of expertise and respect for other beings' business that mortals had abandoned long ago, witches or not. "Do you still have it?"

Jupiter drummed her pink nails on the table. "What's going to happen to us if we hand it over? Are we going to end up dead?"

Emrys raised an eyebrow. "That depends entirely on what it is." He placed his elbows on the table and tried to copy Zackary's customer service smile. "But either way, we came here to stop this thing, including keeping it from harming you or your friends, so we're going to make sure nothing happens to you."

Jupiter studied him, then rummaged through the backpack between her legs beneath the table.

Just opening the bag was enough to freeze Emrys to the spot. Magic poured from whatever she brought out, filling the space like static before a lightning strike and lacing the air with the smell of open water—or was he imagining that? Jupiter sat up and placed a leather-bound book in the center of the table. Emrys snatched it up, unwilling to let its invisible haze of heavy unease touch anyone else. He ran a hand over the black-blue wavy imprints on the cover and shivered, as though staring into the dark depths of the ocean—needing to look up, to surface for air, yet unable to trust that something wouldn't rise from the depths to drag him under.

"Where the hell did they get this?" Emrys whispered.

Jupiter shook her head. "No idea. Collin found it online, I imagine."

Emrys' head snapped up. "I'm sorry, *how* did you end up a coven leader? Performing spells you don't understand from sources you don't know for a pair of magical virgins who have been interested—not practicing, *interested*—in magic for all of five minutes? It's no wonder two people are dead."

"Emrys!" Zackary kicked him under the table. "Enough."

"No, he's right." Jupiter pinched the bridge of her nose. "He's right, I just..." She took a deep, shaky breath. "We wanted to help them. We didn't know how else to do it." She removed her hand and blinked away tears. "There's no real justice in this world for people like us. Not in places like this." She balled up a fist against the table. "You have to either leave shitty towns like this or strong-arm people into being halfway decent, and those aren't always viable options. Spell work feels like the closest thing to having power sometimes, even if we don't always fully understand it. I just wanted to share that with Collin and Ian, but now..." She massaged her temple, her face crumbling around oncoming tears.

Emrys deflated as Sammy put her head on Jupiter's shoulder, and Stone took her free hand. Zackary glowered at him, and Emrys flashed him a dirty look back because it wasn't as if he was wrong. He cleared his throat in an attempt to get the conversation away from his scolding and began to flip through the book. He swore he could hear a whisper with every page he turned. Shivers skittered up his arms as he made out spells and enchantments, most with English pronunciations scribbled above Ancient Greek, Latin, what seemed to be various dialects of Scottish, and Ogham—the old script of Ireland. Whoever had put together this grimoire must have been quite learned, not to mention vindictive. Most of the magic was darker than Emrys was used to seeing, even in Faerieland. There were spells to summon vengeful spirits of the dead. spells to cause deadly accidents, and a charm to be given as a gift that would lead to the wearer choking to death on the next thing they ate.

"And Collin never said who he bought it from?" Emrys asked under his breath, afraid to speak too loud and spook the dark forces tied to the book.

Jupiter shook her head. "I tried to trace it, but I couldn't find any others like it for sale. I think it might have been someone's personal grimoire."

"Can we get to his phone or computer to see where he would have ordered this?"

Stone folded his arms. "The cops still have all that stuff."

Emrys passed a spell designed to make a person hemorrhage to death during menstruation. "Lovely. So, we have a murderous supernatural entity *and* a psychotic human selling fucked up grimoires on the internet on the loose."

Jupiter snorted. "Trust me, we've always had psychotic humans on the loose. Always will. The internet doesn't change that."

The word "siren" caught Emrys' eye. He stopped flipping through pages and read.

His tongue stumbled over the mix of languages as he muttered under his breath, noting the way the witches tensed at the sound. He did his best not to roll his eyes. The spell was useless without proper ritual space, tools, or intent. It would be like trying to start a car on a full tank of gas with no key or wheels.

His gut knotted as he realized that the boys and the coven hadn't been completely off the mark in attempting the spell. The incantation was written to summon a siren to seduce a victim, using her powers to drain away their sexual vitality, but why had the siren come for the boys instead? And why had it ultimately killed them?

Emrys scanned the instructions. "Was the spell performed under the full moon?"

Jupiter nodded. "Yeah. The one in January."

"You threw salt, water, and a shell on the ritual fire?"

"The boys did."

"And the semen? Vaginal fluid? Did you have samples from both the men and the aunt the curse was meant to target?

Zackary choked on his water and thumped himself on the chest as the witches all paled and looked at one another.

"I don't remember reading that." Sammy's face turned bright red. "And I did most of the translating."

"They don't spell it out," Emrys explained. "It's metaphor, talking about 'salt of bodily pleasure to summon the pleasurable salt of the sea'."

"We struggled with that part for weeks," Jupiter chimed in. "We eventually figured out 'salt of the body,' and thought it meant blood. The boys each brought a picture of the people they were cursing and gave a drop of blood. We thought that, since they're blood relations, it should work."

Emrys massaged his temple and took a deep breath, his nostrils flaring as he clenched his jaw to keep himself from commenting "fucking amateurs."

Stone pulled himself further into his hoodie. "Is that what killed them?"

Emrys paused before answering. He didn't need a lecture about tact from Zackary later. "I believe so." He met each of the witches' eyes. "This wasn't a spell to manifest a promotion at work or some sort of confidence booster where you could substitute quartz or a white candle. This was life force magic. It's older, less forgiving, and, most importantly, *binding*. Magic like this doesn't care if you don't know what you're doing. Once you put a part of yourself out there, it's out of your hands, and if it blows up in your face, tough shit. You get what you put in, and a creature like a siren is more than happy to take advantage of a human playing with forces they don't understand. "

Jupiter's shoulders slumped. "So, is that it then? It's over? It won't attack anyone else?"

"I didn't say that." Emrys sat back in his seat and folded his arms, knees bouncing as he thought it over. "The siren still has pictures of the intended victims, right? She could still prey on them if she wanted. Probably is, if the targets are already running around fucking people they're not supposed to and then covering it up." He shrugged. "Personally, I don't think it would be that big of a loss."

Zackary opened his mouth to argue.

Emrys held up a hand to stop him. "*But* we were called up here to do a job, and a job is what we're going to do." He flipped the grimoire shut and got to his feet. "We're taking this." He gave the witches pointed looks. "Stay out of trouble."

Zackary followed behind, the trio trailing after him.

"We made this mess," Jupiter called. "We want to help."

Emrys walked out the door without a single glance back. "You can help by staying out of the way."

The two walked in silence until they reached the car, Emrys rounding it for the passenger seat and Zackary clicking the fob to open the door. "You could have been nicer, you know." There was an edge to his words as he slid into the vehicle. "They just lost their friends, and you were a total—what is it you like to call me? A heavy-handed prick?"

Emrys clicked his seatbelt with more force than necessary. "We're not getting paid to be nice. Besides, they had no business working with magic like that." He snorted and dug his phone from his pocket. "Some coven they turned out to be."

Zackary sighed. "They're just trying to find their way."

Emrys scoffed. "Don't tell me you're defending them."

"No, but I can understand why they do what they do." Zackary ran a hand over his head. "All they've probably known of the spiritual is Christianity, and it's not a faith that values people like them. Not in places like this, but it's where their roots are. Their ties to their ancestors' older faiths are likely long gone. They're trying to find who they are." He turned on the car. "I'm not one of them, but I know what it's like. It can be lonely feeling cut off from anything bigger than yourself."

Emrys studied the demon—the way his face fell, the way his eyes grew distant—and cringed in horror at how he found himself wanting to reach out to him, not out of desire, but out of a need to comfort and apologize.

He wasn't good. He wasn't truly kind or empathetic, so, why did he feel so bad about how he'd talked to those witches? It wasn't as if he was wrong.

He shook the disgusting thought away and pulled up a web browser on his phone. "Didn't know you were such an anthropologist."

Zackary snorted. "That's a big word for you. Do you need to lie down from all the brain power it used?"

Emrys flipped him off as he looked up the next new moon. "Shit, we're going to have to work fast," he said. "If we want to summon this bitch, it's going to have to be tonight. We might not get a chance until next month."

Zackary put the car in reverse. "What do we need to make that happen?"

Emrys smirked. "First, we need to go shopping."

INCENSE DIDN'T IMPACT DEMONS as much as other cleansing herbs like sage or juniper, for which Zackary was grateful as he followed Emrys into the metaphysical store. The scent tickled his nose and scratched his throat, but he'd survive. He studied an array of statues of gods and goddesses from a cornucopia of pantheons as Emrys scanned the displays of stones, muttering to himself as he picked one or two up at a time, then tossed them aside.

Zackary's gaze lingered on a statue of Danu, her eyes downturned and peaceful as she stood draped in robes and flowing hair, a disk decorated with a triskelion in her hands. He knew little of her, besides her name. An Irish summoner of his had tried to call on her once with the help the members of his local Hellfire Club. She hadn't responded and Zackary hadn't blamed her—that club had been a cult of assholes.

Zackary traced the waves of Danu's hair, more impressed with the craftsmanship than he had expected. "Do you ascribe to any particular deities or pantheons, Emrys?"

The pixie weighed a hunk of clear quartz in his hand, then tossed it in his shopping basket. "I don't really think about gods one way or another." He picked through a pile of aquamarine. "They seem to stay well away from my business, so I stay well away from theirs."

"But do you believe in them?"

Emrys shrugged, settled on a stone, and added the rock to his trove. "I guess. Magic has to come from somewhere, I suppose." He stood up straight, scanned the shelves, and then made a beeline for a wall of herbs. He stroked his chin as he looked them over, then took down packages of willow and nettle. "Think Gracie has some salt we can use?"

"I imagine so." Zackary watched as he scanned a display of black screen-printed clothes. After rummaging through a few different designs, he settled on one with a large triquetra in the center and an excited "Oooo" and added it to his basket, making Zackary laugh.

Emrys flashed him a shrewd look. "What?"

"Nothing." Zackary glanced around to ensure they didn't have anyone within earshot. "I just never imagined I'd see a faerie needing tools to perform magic."

Emrys gave an indignant snort and a wry smile. "I can't believe you haven't lorded this little fact over me yet, but I'm not as strong as you. Physically or magically. Outside of glamours and parlor tricks, I never honed the craft. I need conduits for something that requires this much concentration and focus."

Zackary frowned. "I would never lord anything over you, especially something like that."

Emrys studied the demon, his eyes calculating and unreadable, sending a shiver up Zackary's spine. As much as he appreciated the rare occasion that Emrys was serious, he still wasn't sure what to do with them. He preferred to have contingency plans, but he could never nail one down for Serious Emrys.

Zackary cleared his throat and studied a rack of moon-shaped earrings. "Would it be better if I summoned the siren, then? If you give me the instructions, I can handle it. I told you that you don't have to stick around when they show up, and I mean it."

Emrys shook his head and absently took a white candle from a table to his right. "I hate to admit it—because I *really* don't want to do this—but I think you'll only scare them off. Odds are if you command them, they'll come when you call, but they'll hide the whole time. If nothing else, a Hemlock bastard calling them should catch their attention."

Zackary frowned. "I wish you wouldn't call yourself that."

Emrys shrugged and approached the register. He exchanged pleasantries with the girl behind the counter, all but ignoring Zackary until she read the total and he held out his hand toward him.

Zackary looked at Emrys' empty palm and frowned. "Can I help you with something?"

He closed his hand and looked Zackary up and down. "You have a company card from the Order, don't you?"

Zackary snorted. "Yes, but it's for travel and business expenses."

"Um, excuse you." Emrys motioned a circle around the basket with his hand. "What does this look like?"

"Candles, herbs, and rocks."

"Candles, herbs, and rocks for the *business* we were sent to handle." Emrys extended his hand again. "So, card please."

Zackary laughed as he took out his wallet and handed Emrys the credit card with *St. Mary's Interdenominational* in raised letters. "Yes, sir, Mr. Hemlock."

Emrys snatched it from Zackary's hand with a glower. "Consider this sugar daddy practice."

The cashier snorted, then tried to hide it with a cough. Zackary stopped laughing.

Emrys eyed a counter display of sightseeing brochures as the cashier punched the buttons of her small card reader. "Are these free, by chance?" The cashier said they were. Emrys took one dedicated to local camping grounds. With their purchase complete, they walked back to the car. Emrys unfolded the paper to its full-size and scanned the map. He lowered it just long enough to get back in the car and fasten his belt.

Zackary typed Gracie's address into the GPS. "What are you look-ing for?"

"A place for our summoning ritual." Emrys kept his focus glued to the map as Zackary pulled them out of the parking spot.

"Could we ask Jupiter and the others where they performed theirs?"

Emrys shook his head, his dark glamoured hair falling down his face. "I don't trust it. The siren is going to be suspicious enough with me calling them. Using the same spot might send off alarm bells.

Sirens are cunning—they might suspect we're on their tail about the murders."

"Seems like it would be a bit of a stretch for them to make."

"Maybe, but I don't want to take our chances if we've only got this one shot."

Zackary stole glances at Emrys as they drove down the empty highway. Serious Emrys was one thing, but Focused Emrys was a sight to behold like an eclipse. He looked stronger like this—his blue eyes were sharp, calculating, and nearly smoldering as his dark waves fell into his face, his mouth a thin, serious, beautiful line. It was such a contrast against the sass and attitude he'd displayed in the store a moment ago. The image made Zackary chuckle.

Emrys looked up, one eyebrow raised. "What?"

Zackary glanced at his quizzical expression with a smirk. "You know, you're quite funny when you're yourself."

Emrys glared and looked back at the map.

"I'm serious. I don't know if you meant it to be funny but demanding that the Order pay for your pagan trappings has got to be a highlight of the trip for me. You were right, but the way you were right was highly amusing."

Emrys snorted. "Pagan trappings." He sat up straight, leaning against the headrest. "You don't know much about goodfolk magic, do you?"

"I must confess that I don't." Zackary glanced his way. "I'm willing to learn, though."

Emrys was still, turning his head to the window for a long silent moment before speaking. "I don't know if we're pagan in the way humans use the term. Some of us recognize the gods of the Old Ways, but many of their names and domains were either lost or shed when we made our way to this land. In a lot of ways, we're as adrift and peopleless as the humans we hid among—we've been here too long to have anywhere else as home, but our roots are shallow." Emrys folded his arms and leaned his head against the cold glass. "The most American goodfolk can do is draw up magic from the earth and hope for the best. Some of us call on gods for aid, some don't. Some only tap into what we're born with, some grow their craft. All we know is what we are. Magic melts into us the way sunlight melts into plants or the way minerals turn bone to stone. It follows our will like a flock of starlings follows its leader." Emrys untangled his arms to study his right palm, as if reading the lines. "Does that make us pagan? Maybe. I'm not the one to ask, but I know it makes our tools more than 'pagan trappings,' whatever we are, whatever gods may or may not claim us." He folded his arms again and looked Zackary's way. "What about you?"

The demon tensed at the idea of having to follow up Emrys' small monologue. "What about me?"

"Where does your magic come from? Do you truly believe that the god that created you is the only one that can grant power? That has fingerprints on this earth?"

Zackary's jaw clenched and his grip tightened on the wheel. "I hardly see how that's relevant."

"Oh, it's relevant." Emrys sat up straighter with a growing mischievous grin. "You don't get to hide from hard questions after your whole *I'm trying to take you on dates and talk to you so we can fall desperately in love* schtick, so spill."

Zackary's heart raced as heat rose in his face, making him feel ridiculous. "I never said we were falling in love." Emrys didn't mean it. He couldn't.

"Still. I bared a part of myself, so now you owe me."

Zackary shifted in his seat and cleared his throat, daring to remove one hand from the steering wheel to massage the back of his neck. "My magic is a bit more complicated, I think." He placed his hand back on the wheel. "In its truest form, it comes from somewhere inside. Some sort of...miniature sun that I can't exactly pinpoint, but it's always there, burning somewhere in my bones. Being contracted by a human puts up a sort of screen between us that rises and lowers depending on whether I'm doing my master's bidding. Luckily, with Maryam holding my contract, that's not something I really have to worry about. When it comes to gods..."

Zackary drummed on the steering wheel and adjusted the heat before answering. "At one time, I absolutely believed that my Creator was the only being powerful enough to be called a god, but the more time I spent on Earth, the more people I met, and the more supernatural forces I encountered, the less I think that could be true. I may still be Theirs to control and to damn, but there are more beings out there with that sort of power than anyone will ever know, I think."

Emrys fiddled with the passenger-side vent. "Would you trade sides?" he asked softly below the radio. "If it could get you out of Hell?"

Zackary swallowed hard. It would be so easy to lie. Emrys would probably believe him, too—he was steadfast and loyal. Stubborn, even, but Emrys was right. If they were going to finish this mission together, if they were going to be *something* together when this was all over, Zackary would have to give more of himself.

"So long as I could take Maryam with me, yes," he finally answered.

"What do you mean by 'take Maryam with you'?"

"As long as my ties weren't severed to her, as long as I could continue being her godfather, I would walk away in a heartbeat."

Emrys was still. "You really love her, don't you?"

Zackary's heart ached at the faint pain in Emrys' voice. "She's my only daughter left. My only family."

Emrys nodded, his body language smaller, curling in on himself slightly. "How many kids did you have in the beginning?"

"Three." Zackary was startled to find that a lump didn't form in his throat around the words. "A boy and two girls."

"Were you married?"

"To the girls' mother, yes. My son's mother was never interested, but we remained good friends. We all operated like one family in a lot of ways." Zackary flicked on his turn signal to change lanes, maneuvered around an old beat-up truck, and guided the car into the left lane. "You would have liked both of them—my partners."

Emrys snorted. "Yeah, spending time with the women who bore your children wouldn't be intimidating at all."

Zackary brought the car back into the right lane. "Why would that intimidate you? I genuinely think they would have adored you."

Emrys gave him an incredulous look.

"You know, one day, you'll have to start believing the nice things I say about you. I really do mean them."

Emrys shook his head. "Let's take this emotional vulnerability thing one thing at a time, shall we?"

Zackary chuckled. "And we're starting with baring our souls rather than compliments?"

Emrys smirked. "Naturally."

Gracie was less than thrilled with how the conversation with the witches had gone. Zackary couldn't blame her. Jupiter and the others had come to her for help, and Emrys hadn't exactly been tactful with his handling of the situation. Still, she limited her displays of frustration to cross looks, sighs, and a few massages to her temple.

Informing her that they had a plan helped. She pored over the map at the dining room table with Emrys, explaining which trails were closed off for the season, which wound deep into the forest and away from the water, and which would bring them right to the lake.

She paused to pull a venison potpie out of the oven and then came back to trace a red squiggle against the green of the forest. "The clearest trail closest to town is White Tail, but it doesn't let out to the water until you hit a 60-foot sandstone drop. I don't advise trying to cut out the water from the trail before then—the ground is too unstable."

"What about this one? Sparrow Trail?" Emrys pointed to a blue line that snaked through the green.

"Sparrow has less elevation, but it doesn't touch water until it meets up with White Tail about five miles out of town. You won't have to worry about the cliff, but it'll take you longer to get back if something goes wrong. Worse, it could take longer for rescue services to get to you." Gracie slipped off her oven mitts and leaned back against the counter. "I suggest you pick between these two, though. Even with a few of the other trails not being shut down, they're going to have more snow."

Emrys folded his hands in front of his mouth, his gaze downcast and eyebrows furrowed. Finally, he looked to Zackary on his left and asked, "What are your thoughts?"

Zackary took a long, slow sip of his tea as he thought everything over—both their options and the fact that Emrys had genuinely asked his opinion on the matter. "My vote is for Sparrow. If you go over that cliff and I can't snatch you, or if I go over and I'm too injured to fly, it won't matter how close or far we are to town—we're fucked." He winced. "I mean, we're in trouble."

Gracie chuckled and topped off her neat whiskey. "I'm a big girl. I can take bad words."

"Force of habit." Zackary took another sip of tea. "My goddaughter's aunt is a stickler for language."

Gracie ticked up an eyebrow as she laced her fingers around the glass. "Anyone I know?"

"Maybe. Sarah Bishop? Married to Hiro Bishop?"

Gracie sipped her whiskey and thought, slowly licking her lips before answering. "She grew up in St. Bishop's Orphanage, I take it?"

"They both did, yeah."

Gracie nodded, then watched her glass as she slowly swirled the ice and liquor. "I might know her." Her eyes seemed to go a bit distant. "It's a common name though, especially in the Order."

Zackary almost asked. He almost reached for his phone to pull up a picture of the Bishop family in the hopes that he could jog her memory and possibly get an answer to the question that stuck to the back of his mind like a scab, itching and begging to be picked at. But picking scabs drew blood, and Zackary only had the mental bandwidth to deal with one mess at a time.

Emrys' voice cut through his internal musing. "Sparrow Trail it is, then."

Zackary turned toward him. "You don't want to argue for White Tail?"

Emrys shrugged. "Why would I? Your argument made sense. We can't solve this problem if we freeze to death." A smirk crept to his lips. "Besides, we're supposed to be trusting each other, aren't we? I trust you on this."

Zackary's brain came up short with a response, argument or otherwise. He was too busy trying to process the way his heart had begun to race, sending heat to his face. He turned away, bringing his mug to his lips.

Emrys laughed. "What? I only get your little compliments when I bait you?"

"Get any smart ideas, and I'll bait you right off that cliff. How about that?"

Gracie chuckled and turned towards the cupboard behind her, opened it, and began to take out plates. "Stop pecking at each other, and help me set the table." She set the plates down in front of Zackary. "You can't go chasing sirens in the dark on an empty stomach."

Hours later, on the icy black cold of the trail, Zackary had to agree with Gracie—the warm meal they had eaten seemed like the only source of heat left in the world. Gracie had insisted Zackary borrow cold weather gear an old boyfriend had left behind—Emrys borrowed Gracie's—but the clothes didn't seem to lend any heat. They merely staved off the cold as best they could. By the time they reached the secluded beach, the tips of Zackary's toes and fingers had started to go numb. Why the hell had humans settled in this desolate place? If *he* was beginning to feel the elements, they had no business settling here year-round.

Zackary fell into step behind Emrys as he crossed the snowy sand, stopping right in the center, a few steps from the frozen shoreline. He went to work, digging his tools from his backpack. Zackary put away his flashlight and channeled what little heat was left in his body to call forth an orb of light so that Emrys could work, laying out the cloth, crystal, herbs, and candles. When Emrys asked Zackary to use the kindling they had brought to build a small fire, leaving enough space between the makeshift altar and the flames for Emrys to sit, he did so, no questions asked. Truth be told, he was grateful for the task and the heat it provided once he had it lit with the same energy that gave them light.

Emrys took his seat before the altar and pulled a charcoal pencil from his pocket. "Put that out."

Zackary obeyed and watched in the flickering light as Emrys drew the point-down triangle that symbolized water on his palms. He then took a water bottle from the bag, poured it into a small ceramic basin Gracie had lent him, and then tossed the bag and bottle to the side, just out of reach.

He dug his phone out of his pocket. "Don't laugh at me for this." He gave Zackary a shrewd look.

Zackary lifted his hands in surrender. "Hey, this is your magic. Do what you need to do."

Emrys looked slightly doubtful, but he navigated through the screen until a faint, steady, deep drumbeat came from the speakers. He turned the sound up and gently set his phone aside. "It helps me focus. Like I said, I've never really honed the craft."

"Like I said, this is all you. I trust you."

Emrys settled into his seat, rolled his neck, closed his eyes, and sat up tall, his palms up. "Stand behind the fire. Don't move until I do."

Zackary moved to his position, crouched, and watched as Emrys began to sway, nodding in time with the drums, mumbling words in a language of few vowels, musical rhythms, and consonants pronounced further back in the mouth than those of English. Some were consonants not heard in English at all. With a shiver, Zackary realized he was listening to Old Fae—a language endowed with more magic than words.

Emrys threw herbs and salt into the basin in rhythm with the drums as he chanted, his voice growing louder and more forceful, an image of another world neither fully known on Earth nor ever in Hell. Zackary couldn't look away, hypnotized by the sound, movement, and scent of herbs and burning wood until a form took shape on the ice.

He lowered his gaze, frozen in place as the shape of a woman emerged from the dark with slow, dainty steps that swayed her hips. Her face was still hidden in shadow, and her long, wet hair matched the starless night. The firelight snagged on her sharp features as she neared—her slender nose, angular lips, and pointed chin. His heart hammered as she came ever closer, a savage, hungry smile spreading across her mouth.

A cry for Emrys to move built in Zackary's throat. Emrys' ritual stopped before Zackary could release it. Emrys scrambled away, nearly crawling into the fire as the figure took her first steps onto the snowy sand with bare feet.

There she stood still, the only sound being the beating of drums and the crackling of fire as the icy wind tugged at the naked woman's limp, soaked hair. Zackary's heart hammered as she raised her face just enough to look down the length of her nose at Emrys, the firelight setting her eyes ablaze.

Her smile turned bloodthirsty as she said, "Hello, lover."

That voice. That face.

They made Emrys want to scream, run, and throw up all at the same time, and yet they brought him out of his body somehow, as if his soul were outside of space, back in a time when that face had been everything to him, and then everything he feared and despised as his world burned down around him.

Nyxara's head tilted to the side as she raised an eyebrow—a familiar sign to Emrys that she was amused, but she didn't want you to know *how* amused. "Of all the men I've loved, you're the last one I ever expected to call me again." She let out a low, knowing chuckle. Emrys' stomach churned at the memory of how that sound used to make heat pool in his core.

The slow-growing heat of the fire finally nipped his neck hot enough to snap him out of his daze. He snatched his phone from the sand and turned off the audio as he scrambled to his feet and backed up toward Zackary.

The demon's hands steadied him as the two of them collided. "Emrys, who is this?"

Nyxara's dark eyes glinted in the firelight as she looked Zackary up and down. She gave a mock pout and placed her hands on her hips, thrusting them to the side. "Aw, is this your new toy, darling? Glad to see you haven't lost your sense of taste." She flashed her sharp teeth in a hungry grin. "Mind if I have a bite? You've always been so good at sharing."

Rage bloomed in Emrys' chest. He took a step forward, shoulders back to build space between Zackary and Nyxara. "Stay the fuck away from him."

Nyxara threw her head back and laughed. "Still bitter about the business with the queen?" Her eyes narrowed, her expression shifting to that of a smug cat with a cornered canary. "Or was it the fire?"

"Enough." Emrys reached down and grabbed a branch from the fire, the end carrying weak, dancing flames as the structure collapsed in on itself. "Did you kill Collin Johnson and Ian Phillips, or do you know who did?"

Nyxara scoffed, then studied her nails. "Why? Are the mortals bothered?"

Emrys snarled, his grip tightening on the branch. "You took them from their families—their *futures*, you hard-hearted bitch."

Nyxara's eyes turned to murderous slits, her body stiffening. There was a time when that change in body language would have scared Emrys. Hell, it probably still should have scared him, but too much hatred tinted his vision. She had taken too much—*destroyed* too much, both then and now, for him to feel anything rational like fear.

He had been so sure he would run if it was her. Zackary had even given him an out, but learning the truth, knowing the depth of hurt and betrayal Collin and Ian had faced only to wind up dead, filled Emrys with a rage that rooted him to the spot.

Zackary stepped around Emrys, holding out an arm to slow him. "Let's all just breathe, okay? This doesn't have to get messy." Emrys hated how level his voice was, how calm and controlled it was. "My name is Zackary Bishop. I work for the Rosary Order down in Detroit. We're here to investigate the potential murders of two humans. We were told that this book"—Zackary motioned to the grimoire lying on the sand—"was used in a ritual to summon a siren to punish the boys' families for having an affair."

Nyxara tittered, covering her mouth with one hand. "Is *that* why I've been seeing images of three sad old mortals in my head for the last month? I was supposed to kill *them*?" She gave a mocking snap of her fingers. "Damn." She shrugged. "That's what humans get for messing with magic, I guess."

Zackary went rigid. "So, you admit that you were the one to kill the boys?"

Nyxara smirked. "I did what their spell asked me to and took my payment." She absently brushed the string of jagged, broken shells and stones at her neck. "Nothing more, nothing less."

"So, you believed the boys and their friends performed that spell because they *wanted* to die?"

Nyxara raised an eyebrow, her mouth turned down in annoyance. "I didn't *believe* anything about them, handsome. They performed a spell requesting my particular...gifts." Nyxara slid one hand down the side of her hip. "And they gave their blood—a sign that they were willing to pay in blood. It's not my fault they messed up the spell."

"Don't play innocent." Emrys' empty hand tightened into a fist. "Why them? Why bother? You never bothered with mortals before."

Nyxara shrugged. "I was passing through and wound up ensnared in the spell. What would you have me do?" She motioned to the twinkling lights of Glace in the distance. "Hang around that shithole until they died of old age, and I was free? I'm a busy woman."

"Bull-fucking-shit." Emrys caught the way Zackary tensed at his volume, but he didn't care. "You could have worked with those kids. You could have *talked* to them, but instead, you saw an excuse to take advantage of someone weaker than you, just like you always do."

Nyxara rolled her eyes. "Oh, come off it, Emrys. I didn't make you stay in my bed any longer than you wanted to, and breakups happen." She studied the back of her nails. "It just so happens that our breakup held the promise of the Hemlock queen's favor and a *lot* of money."

"*You miserable cunt!*"

"Hey!" Zackary held him back, pinning Emrys in place with a glare. Emrys blinked away the red in his vision and discovered he was several feet from where he had been standing. When had he lunged forward?

Zackary faced Nyxara again. "Ma'am, we're going to need you to come with us."

Nyxara scoffed. "And why would I do that?"

"Because we can't just let you walk away from what you've done. There have to be consequences."

Nyxara lowered her hands to her sides. As she slowly brought them up again, a devilish, hungry smile spread across her face as slender pillars of water cracked through the ice and towered above her, waiting for her next command. "So sorry, handsome," she said. "But I don't answer to the false god's castouts."

Emrys had seen that move before. "Move!" He shoved Zackary out of her line of fire and hit the sand as one of her whips struck the fire, putting it out with a hiss. The other embedded itself in the sand where Emrys had stood, its form now frozen in a spear of ice. Emrys scrambled to his feet and snatched up the branch.

Zackary reached for him as he got to his feet. "Emrys, wait!"

Fuck that. He had waited nearly fifty years already.

Ice crunched beneath his feet as he swung for her face. Her gaze snapped his way with a grin as she willed another flash of water from the lake towards Emrys. He bat it away in an explosion of frigid water. A blade of ice sliced through his coat, nicking his arm. He hissed and swung for Nyxara's arm. She slid out of the way, gliding over the ice toward the depths of Lake Superior like a phantom as she cackled.

"Look how much you've grown up, Emrys," she called. "Last time I saw you, you only knew how to run away."

Before Emrys could snarl back that Nyxara only knew how to suck dick, a flash of light caught his eye as it shot across the water, cutting off Nyxara's escape. She whirled and halted as a blade of sunbeams and solar flares came down in front of her.

It could have sliced her in two, had Zackary really meant it.

Emrys knew him, though. Even in this bright, winged, glowing form, he had wanted to give Nyxara a warning—a chance to stand down and come quietly instead of meeting oblivion. It was more than she deserved, even before she killed those two human boys, but he wouldn't know that. Emrys hadn't warned him because he was a coward.

"Don't make us hurt you." Zackary's ethereal voice sent a ripple over the icy water.

Nyxara smirked over her shoulder toward Emrys. "Something tells me I don't have to *make* Emrys try to hurt me."

Emrys' teeth ground together as he imagined all the ways he'd like to rip her apart if they had the time.

"Did he ever tell you about me?" She turned back to Zackary. "Has he shown you any of the little tricks I taught him? If he has, you're welcome—he was clueless before he stumbled into my bed."

"Fifty fucking years and you've yet to learn how to shut up, Nyx," Emrys called.

She turned with a smug smirk. "Fifty years and you're still that scared little boy in the cupboard, waiting for your chance to run."

He'd told her about that in confidence, back when he was still hers and she had sheltered him from the world of Faerieland—a world that only saw him as a trick, a toy, or a paycheck, and she'd thrown it back in his face. She'd thrown his *mother's death* in his face.

Something beneath his breastbone shattered, flooding him with a torrent of thick, molten rage. He took a step into the shallows. The ice and water skittered away, parting for him, leaving a clear path of sand where he walked. Heat licked his fingertips from nowhere. He gripped the branch in his hand and the end ignited. There was no room in his mind for questions. No room for wonder or joy. There was only a burning need to finish what Nyxara had started fifty years ago, flames and all.

The siren's expression fell, her pale face blanched to bone white as Emrys approached through the frozen lake on dry land.

The look brought a grin to Emrys' face. "Who's running, bitch?" Nyxara snarled.

Zackary seized the moment of distraction, snatching her by the arm. She whipped a wave spiked with ice in his face. Zackary stumbled. Nyxara summoned a tendril of water, sharpening it to a spear of ice, aimed for Zackary's exposed jugular. Emrys charged, bringing his makeshift weapon down on her with a scream of fury and pain.

Nyxara whirled and raised a shield of ice. It cracked under Emrys' blow. He swung from the side, knocking Nyxara off-balance. She shrieked in frustration, firing a needle of ice across Emrys' face. He stumbled back, then swiped low. Nyxara tried to run him through from above. Emrys dove out of the way, catching a glimpse of Zackary bringing his sword down on her arm.

Nyxara's hand came free of her wrist as if Zackary had merely sliced through paper. She shrieked and cradled the stump to her chest, whipping her remaining hand every which way, firing strike after strike of water and ice until Emrys could hardly see. Through the onslaught, he made out Nyxara growing smaller as she backed away towards the deeper waters. No. Emrys might have been the one to run last time, but he would not let this go unfinished again. With a cry and a flash of his sword, Zackary slicked through the sea of attacks, clearing a path. Emrys took it, charging forward despite Zackary's cries to wait. Emrys screamed for Nyxara, pouring out every ounce of pain and betrayal that had festered in the last fifty years. She looked over her shoulder with the deepest look of hatred and bloodlust Emrys had ever seen.

She flicked her wrist.

A sharp pain sliced across Emrys' neck, the tendril so small and fast that he missed it.

So sharp that it was gone before he even tried to breathe, only to get a windpipe full of blood.

Zackary's world stopped turning. He watched Emrys reach for his throat as it turned to a river of red, his eyes bulging and his mouth gaping as the water rushed in around him, his power bleeding out like his life. His knees gave out as the water swallowed his shins. Zackary shot forward and caught him before the water could take him, flying them both back to shore so fast that Zackary's eyes watered against the wind.

Emrys wheezed and flailed, his bugged eyes searching the water. "Go...Go...After—"

Zackary clamped one hand over the wound, the other over Emrys' heart to make sure it kept beating. "Shut the fuck up and hold still." He held so tight to Emrys' neck that his palm stuck to it with the hot blood seeping through his fingers. Zackary focused on breathing in through his nose, out through his mouth as he willed his cosmic energy, magic older than time itself, to knit together cartilage and flesh. If he didn't, the smell and sight of blood and the fear on Emrys' face would send him spiraling, and he'd lose him.

He couldn't lose him. He couldn't lose anyone else. Not Emrys. Not like this.

The fight went out of Emrys' eyes, and they drooped.

Zackary took his hand from Emrys' chest and tapped him on the cheek. "Em! Em, stay with me. Look at me."

Emrys struggled and began losing his fight to keep his eyes open.

"Do you want to hear about how I lost my virginity?"

Emrys' gaze flickered to Zackary's face.

Zackary almost laughed in relief and turned his gaze back to Emrys' neck. "Her name was Tiamat. Her father was a cruel man, looking for every way to cheat those around him out of coins or wears, so naturally, in those days, having three daughters was a problem to him."

Emrys convulsed as he let out a fit of coughs, spitting a mouthful of blood and then taking a raspy but full breath.

"Stay still." Zackary kept his hand where it was. "I need to make sure this is strong enough not to rip the second you stand up."

Emrys managed a weak nod.

"Anyway, I don't remember how he did it, but he got the king of his city to pay him a pretty penny to take Tia as a concubine. She wasn't having it. When she told her father, he held a knife to her throat and said he'd kill her if she didn't go through with it. That night, she drugged her family so she could slip away—not enough to kill them, but enough that they'd sleep late into the morning, and she'd be long gone before they realized what had happened.

"Even then, we were outsiders. People said we were dark magicians. Men possessed by evil spirits, but Tiamat laughed and danced when she reached our camp as if she had reached the promised land. We told her she was safe. We told her no one would dare take her from us. She said that wasn't enough. She said she needed to lose what her father had promised the king. She pointed to me and said, 'You. You will do.'"

A smile tugged at Emrys' lips.

"I knew what she meant, of course. Other humans had joined us and my brothers had been more than willing to experiment with their new mortal bodies. She took me by the hand and led me to a nearby grove. When I protested, she asked if I wished to stop. I told her no, just that I was inexperienced. She said she didn't care. That she would do all the work. She did...for the whole two minutes that it lasted."

Emrys let out a laugh that morphed into a yelp of pain. His face crumpled into pain, and his hand shot atop Zackary's.

"Sorry! Sorry. I should've picked a different story."

A smirk tugged at Emrys' lips as he dropped his hand. "Oh, no," he wheezed. "This one was absolutely worth staying alive for."

Zackary snorted, a bit of tension melting from his body as relief seeped into his taut muscles. "She wasn't bothered, though. She got up, went to bathe in the nearby river, then settled among the humans that had joined us as if our little clan had always been her home." Beneath his hand, Zackary could feel the new fibers of Emrys' body settle into place, woven among the old. "She must not have been too put off because she came looking for my bed on a regular basis after that." He took his hand from Emrys' neck and studied the fresh, puckered scar against his green skin. "Three years later, she bore my son."

Emrys brought his fingers to the scar, his eyes calculating as he watched Zackary's face. "What was his name?"

It was heavy on Zackary's tongue, weighed down by grief as old as the earth yet lighter than Zackary expected. He had never been able to pull his son's name from the depths of his broken heart before. "Ramman."

Emrys swallowed with a wince, then moved to sit up, only to falter.

"Careful." Zackary caught him, steadying him as he propped himself up on his elbow. "Take it easy." He slipped one arm around Emrys' shoulders, dipped the other under his knees, and lifted him off the ground.

Emrys tried to crane his neck to look over Zackary's shoulder at the water, only to wince and settle his head against his shoulder. "You should have gone after her."

"Don't be thick. You would have died."

"We had a job to do."

"That job isn't worth your life. We're not leaving until she's taken care of, but losing you wouldn't have brought those boys back."

Emrys curled in on himself in Zackary's arms. "The world would keep turning without me."

Zackary remembered watching the sun rise the morning after his wife and daughters had been slaughtered. The way it rose after he'd found his son dead, after the deaths of all the fragile mortals he'd made the mistake of getting close to. "Maybe," he said. "But the light would be dimmer. Duller." Zackary held him tighter. "Let's get you back to Gracie's. We need to get your blood sugar up and keep you warm." He braced himself, stretched his wings, and shot into the air.

Emrys buried his face in Zackary's coat against the wind.

Zackary shot across the water toward the lights of Glace, following the glow to the familiar downtown street they had driven that morning. He traced the road into the grid of woods and barren farmland, spying the black roof of Gracie's house just as the porch light flickered on and the front door opened.

Odin and Zeus darted into the night, spotting Zackary above, barking and leaping as if he had introduced some sort of game. Gracie rushed to join her dogs, craning her neck and squinting into the dark sky, mouth agape as Zackary descended to the snowy yard, covered in Emrys' blood like an angel of death.

Gracie's awe turned to panic at the sight of Emrys, limp and gory, in Zackary's arms. She distracted the dogs by launching a stick, then rushed to meet them, hands reaching for Emrys. "What on earth happened?"

Zackary angled Emrys so that Gracie could get a better look at him. "It was a siren that killed the boys. Someone Emrys knew. When we confronted her, she attacked and slit his throat. I was able to stitch him back together, but he's lost a lot of blood."

Gracie paled as she gingerly pulled back the hem of his coat to study the newly formed scar. "You poor thing."

Emrys managed a weak smirk. "'Tis only a scratch."

Worry stayed etched on Gracie's face as she ushered them into the house. "Take him upstairs. There are washed clothes in the center closet. I'll be up in a minute."

Zackary obeyed, maneuvering Emrys up the steps and into the bathroom, setting him on the closed toilet. "Don't move."

Emrys gave a tired thumbs-up as Zackary dashed into the hall, grabbed a cloth from the closet, and then came back to wet the scar with warm water and Jupiter-scented soap from the tub. He winced as Zackary dabbed at his injuries.

Sorry. Is the water too hot?"

It's fine. Skin's just tender."

Zackary ran the cloth under the faucet again, streaking the tub red and pink as he wrung it out. He inspected the scar, grateful that the faint puckered green line looked weeks old already, then worked to get Emrys out of his bloody shirt.

The pixie shivered. This is not how I wanted the first time you took my clothes off to go."

Zackary snorted as he gently scrubbed away the drying blood on his chest. "How are you feeling?"

Emrys shrugged. "Dizzy. Cold."

We'll get you some broth and something to drink once you're in bed. You need fluids, salt, and sugar. Vitamins, if Gracie has any."

Emrys nodded.

They fell into silence as Zackary worked to wipe away the blood, his stomach rolling at the realization of just how much Emrys had lost. Emrys shivered as the cooling cloth met the back of his neck, and Zackary's fingers ached to trace the faint muscles beneath green skin, needing to feel he was alive.

Being cross with Emrys was always a good distraction from how much Zackary wanted to touch him.

Why didn't you let me handle this?" he asked with no real fire in his voice. I told you that you didn't have to do this if it was someone you knew."

Emrys weakly shook his head. "I wanted to. I couldn't..." He swallowed, wincing at the motion. "I wanted to make her suffer for what she did to Collin and Ian. What she did to me." He stole a glance at Zackary. "And I didn't want her to hurt you."

Zackary nudged Emrys to turn so he could reach his back. He winced at the sight of blood and sand caked into Emrys' dark curls. "We're gonna have to put you in the shower. Your hair is a mess."

"Think you can handle yourself?"

Zackary rolled his eyes at the smirk in Emrys' voice. "Just take off your pants."

"You have no idea how long I've waited to hear you say those words."

"Keep it up, and I'm waterboarding you." Zackary helped Emrys out of the rest of his clothes and into the shower, where he sat while Zackary took down the shower head and adjusted the temperature.

As he wet Emrys' hair, he said, "Tell me everything."

Emrys was still for a moment as his hair plastered against his forehead under the stream of water, his eyes distant and brow furrowed. We met at a party and fell into bed together," he finally said. "In the morning, she insisted I stay. I didn't have anywhere else to go at the time, so I did. As time went by, it seemed like she wanted me around for *me*, not just for the sex. She was the first person who seemed to want to be around me just because, instead of seeing me as a pretty toy to fuck or a pair of horns that could be cut off for the Hemlock queen's favor."

Emrys shoulders slumped forward. "But, in hindsight, I think I must have been wrong because the sex got...darker over time. Rougher. Harder." He wrapped his arms around himself. "I think she was just being kind to get me to try whatever she wanted. The one time I told her to stop, things...changed."

Zackary's stomach knotted around a wave of nausea. "Did she—"

"She never forced me. Coerced, maybe? I don't know. I don't like to think about it." His fingers dug into the skin of his arms. "But giving a hard no was a deal breaker for her. One night, I woke up to find her missing. I was worried, so I went looking to find her and found her talking to...someone...about how it was time to turn me in to the Hemlock queen." Emrys swallowed hard with a wince. "She said if I wasn't going to be useful in bed, the least I could do was be useful to her coin purse. That power I used on the beach manifested itself for the first time and helped me escape. I haven't used it since. I keep it locked away as best I can."

Zackary focused on his breathing. He worried he might shatter the plastic shower head if he didn't. He traced back through Emrys' words, looking for something, *anything* that would distract him from how violently he wanted to rip that bitch apart.

"When you said she told someone, you paused." Zackary set the shower head in its cradle and reached for a bottle of shampoo.

Emrys froze.

Zackary poured some into his hands before massaging it into Emrys' hair. "Emrys, who had she told?"

"It doesn't matter."

Zackary paused, his fingers deep in a lather. "Emrys, if there's someone she'd call for backup, we need to—"

"She can't." Emrys closed his eyes and shook his head. "He's dead." Emrys' hands tightened to fists on his thighs. He took a few deep breaths, then looked up at Zackary, his gaze like a dog ready to be beaten. "It was our other partner." He swallowed hard. "Nyx already had someone when I met her."

Zackary blinked.

"Monogamy in Faerieland is something the powerful use to concentrate influence and secession," Emrys continued. "Common folk don't care quite as much. We were only friends at first, but..." Emrys licked his lips. "Zack, please say something. You're killing me."

Zackary finally let out a soft chuckle as he gently steered Emrys' head forward again so that he could finish washing his hair. "I'm a celestial entity damned for all eternity for taking human lovers and siring half-mortal children. What makes you think I would judge you for something like that?"

"I don't know." Emrys dropped his gaze as Zackary tilted his head back. "You're just so...*good*."

"Loving more than one person at a time doesn't make you bad, Emrys. You aren't bad *at all*. I keep trying to tell you, but you refuse to listen. Tip your head back."

Emrys didn't reply. He simply complied as Zackary rinsed his hair, conditioned it, then rinsed it again.

Have you ever been in a relationship like that?" he asked as Zackary left to grab a towel.

Once or twice." Zackary eased Emrys to his feet, helped him dry off, then bundled him in the towel before scooping him up and carrying him into the bedroom with the queen-sized bed. He sat him down and cupped Emrys' face so he couldn't look away. "Thank you for telling me. I'm so sorry they hurt you. We're going to make sure Nyx never hurts anyone again."

Emrys nodded, color rising in his cheeks. He wriggled away to dry his hair better and smirked as he looked around the bed. "Are you expecting a reward for saving my life?"

Heat touched Zackary's face, and he walked away. "Don't start. You'll be more comfortable here, and you need proper rest."

Mm-hm."

Zackary ignored him as he walked to Emrys' original guest room and dug through his backpack for clothes.

There's plenty of room in here if you change your mind."

Zackary whipped the clothes at him from the doorway. Get into bed. I'll go get the car."

He shut the door and made his way down the hall, meeting Gracie on the stairs. In her hand, she held a tray stacked with cut honeydew,, hot tea, and a large glass of a brightly colored sports drink.

He gave her a tired smile, tension leaving his body with the reminder that he wasn't alone. Thank you, Gracie. I'm going to get the car. I put Emrys in the bigger bedroom if that's okay."

"That's fine." She looked Zackary over. "Are you sure you're okay to drive?"

"Of course."

Gracie frowned. Your hands are shaking, Zackary."

He looked down. Sure enough, they were trembling. He gave Gracie another smile as he slipped his hands in his pockets. I'll be okay. The cold air will clear my head before I get behind the wheel." He slipped past her on the stairs and headed for the door before she could ask more questions, steadying himself with a pat on the dogs' heads.

The car sat where Zackary had left it, coated in a fine dusting of snow that had started to fall. He unlocked it, slipped inside, and leaned his head against the headrest as it began to warm up.

Violent images blinded him the second he closed his eyes—his youngest daughter impaled on an angel's spear, his wife's body face down in the dirt with their eldest strewn on top of her, a knife in her back.

Zackary drew a deep, shaky breath and dug the hilt of his palms into his eyes, his fingernails clawing into his forehead.

Ramman's blank eyes, milky with death, staring up at the merciless heavens from a pike.

Humans pulled apart by their limbs. Beheaded. Disemboweled. Fallen angels skinned. Burning alive.

Matthew's dead body chained to a radiator. Maryam bleeding out in the tub.

Emrys gasping for air as his throat filled with blood, the light going out in his eyes.

FUCK!" Zackary slammed his hands on the steering wheel. "GOD FUCKING DAMN IT!" His scream devolved into broken cries as he dropped his head against the steering wheel, his shoulders shaking as they buckled under everyone he had failed, everyone he had hurt, and everyone he would never see again in his long immortal life.

The sun will still rise without me.

It would, forever bathing Zackary in the light of his failures, in the light of the God and the angels who made sure his punishment—his damnation—never ended, whether he was on Earth or in Hell.

Gods, it had been so long. Why wouldn't they just end him already?

Eventually, Zackary couldn't tell how long, his sobs eased into shaky breaths, his body numb and brain fuzzy as it fizzled out to silence.

The high trumpet melody of *The Godfather Waltz* played from his phone. He lifted and wiped his face, knowing it was Maryam calling—she loved to change her ringtone to that damn song whenever Zackary wasn't looking.

He answered the call, putting it on speaker. "Hey, sweetheart. Everything okay?"

Maryam yawned on the other end. "Yeah. You didn't call when you landed."

"I'm sorry. We got straight to work." Zackary checked the time. "Why are you up? It's one in the morning."

"Trouble sleeping. The apartment feels weird without you and Emrys here." She paused. Are you okay? You sound off."

Zackary massaged his temple. Crying always left him with a headache. "Tired. It was a long day."

"Did you find the killer?"

"We did. Catching her is going to take more work than we thought. We've got it under control, though."

Maryam yawned again. "Okay. I'll let you go to bed. I just wanted to check on you." She paused. "And I know we don't really talk about our feelings, but you should know my life wouldn't be half as good as it is without you in it. Hell, without you, I don't think I'd be alive." She paused. "I'm very grateful for you, Zack."

Zackary's throat tightened. He squeezed his eyes shut, desperate not to cry again. If Maryam knew Emrys was hurt, she'd be in Glace by morning. "I'm grateful for you too, Maryam May."

"G'night, Zack."

"G'night, sweetheart." He waited for her to hang up, clicked off his screen, and leaned his head on the steering wheel, his body still tired and empty but lighter.

The house was dark when Zackary pulled into the driveway. Gracie had texted him where to find the spare key on the porch, so he let himself in on tiptoe. Thor and Zeus growled from their beds by the fireplace but quieted and wagged their tails once Zackary whispered that all was well. He crept up the creaky stairs, ready to drop on his bed and fall asleep in his clothes, but a quick glance in the bathroom mirror reminded him that he was still streaked with blood. Zackary dragged himself into the shower, washed off, and slipped into clean sweats, if for no other reason than to keep Gracie's sheets clean.

Excited muttering caught his ear as he crossed the hall back to his room, drawing him toward Emrys' closed door. He lightly knocked, then eased the door open to find Emrys curled up in bed, his sleeping face bathed in blue light. Zackary allowed himself a small smile as he padded into the room, gingerly picked up the phone, and turned off the video.

Emrys stirred and stretched, his expression dazed and pinched as he blinked in the dark. "I was watching that."

"You need rest."

Emrys sat up and rubbed his eyes. "I wanted to make sure you got home okay."

"Well, I did." Zackary turned to leave. "Now go to sleep."

"Please stay."

Zackary stopped, caught off guard by the desperation in Emrys voice. Zackary didn't think he had ever heard Emrys say please before.

He turned and watched as a thousand different feelings played across Emrys' face as he bit his bottom lip.

"Please?" he repeated. "I don't want to be alone right now." He dropped his gaze, wringing the edge of the comforter. "Every time I close my eyes, I'm scared my throat's going to open again, and I won't be able to call for you. I know it's stupid, but—"

Zackary walked back to the edge of the bed. "It's not stupid." He lifted the covers. "Scooch."

Emrys did, making room for Zackary to slip into bed. Before he could turn on his side, facing the edge, Emrys burrowed down in the blankets and placed his head on Zackary's chest, his arm draped over his middle. Every fiber in Zackary's body caught fire, every neuron firing at the same time at the sensation of Emrys' legs tangling with his and the rhythm of his breath.

Well, fuck. Now he wasn't sleeping either.

He tried to make sense of what was happening—the heat beneath his skin and the pounding in his ears. Emrys had almost died. He needed rest and quiet. This wasn't about Zackary and his terror that he'd be responsible for yet another death. He needed to calm down and go the fuck to sleep.

But Emrys was alive. He was warm and breathing and so close. What if he had died on that beach and Zackary had never gotten to see him again? What if he never had the chance to listen to his stupid jokes or fight off his flirting or—

"Your heart's beating fast," Emrys muttered in the dark.

Zackary swallowed hard as his mouth went dry. "It's just...hard to settle."

Emrys traced absent circles against Zackary's ribs, making him shiver.

"If you had died..." Zackary's arm tightened around Emrys. "Gods, Emrys, it would have broken me. I can't lose anyone else. If I lose anyone else, I'll—"

"Hey." Emrys sat up, twisting to look Zackary in the eye. "Don't. You didn't lose me. I'm right here." He blinked. "And did you just reference the gods?" He chuckled. "Now who's a pagan?"

"Well, someone was on our side tonight, and it's well-established that the *God* god hates me."

"No. You saved me. *You.*" Emrys poked Zackary in the chest for emphasis. "And..." His hand fanned out against Zackary's sweatshirt as he looked for the words. "And I'm grateful."

Zackary couldn't breathe. He couldn't move. All he could do was watch the faint trace of Emrys' tongue across his bottom lip, his eyes on Zackary's mouth. "Don't," Zackary whispered. "Don't do this just because I saved you."

Emrys leaned in close. "We both know that's not what's happening." His breath brushed over Zackary's face. He wanted nothing more than to steal it away.

"I'll still be here in the morning." His gaze flickered to Zackary's. "I promise."

Zackary raised his head, his mouth brushing Emrys' lips, because he couldn't stay in a world where he didn't know every inch of Emrys Hemlock, sharing breath and touch and heat.

So, Zackary kissed him.

Emrys' lips met his, hungry and hunting, his tongue prodding beyond Zackary's teeth as Zackary tangled his hands in Emrys' hair, locking the two of them together, all but praying they could meld together. Emrys moaned into Zackary's mouth, turning Zackary's low core to molten heat. Zackary pulled away just enough to start planting kisses along his jaw, his hands sliding under Emrys' shirt and up his back. Emrys' breath hitched as he pressed into Zackary, shifting his legs to fit with Zackary's and brushing right up against the hard length between his legs.

Zackary froze in mute terror, his face beginning to burn as Emrys pulled back with a satisfied smirk.

"I-I'm sorry." Zackary hid his face in his hands. "We should stop."

Emrys chuckled low and sultry in his chest, only making things worse. "Seems like we're just getting started."

"You need to rest."

Emrys pressed a kiss to Zackary's collarbone. "I can rest after." His fingers brushed against Zackary's waistband. "Let me touch you."

Zackary bit back a moan as Emrys massaged his hip, slow and deep. What was the problem again?

Emrys kissed lower with a smile against Zackary's skin. "Besides, it'll only take me two minutes, right?"

Some deep, dormant part of Zackary snapped awake—lust like a hungry maw, starving after centuries of sleep. He grabbed Emrys by his hair, forcing his head back. "Careful, princeling." Emrys' eyes fluttered as Zackary held on tighter, turning Zackary's blood to jet fuel. "I can't be rough with you right now, but I can still teach you a lesson."

"Teach me, then." Emrys slipped his hand deeper into Zackary's sweats, his fingers wrapping around him as his gaze locked with Zackary's. "I'm all yours."

Emrys had never woken up to a room full of sunlight after having sex before. He was always up, dressed, and out the door before dawn, yet the height of the sun told him that the morning had started hours ago. He turned to find Zackary's side of the bed empty. Being the one to sleep in was a first. At least, it was since...

Emrys balled a handful of the sheets in a fist. Nyxara was here. *She* was the problem, and Emrys' lingering feelings about how things had ended had nearly gotten him killed. He shifted onto his back and stared up at the ceiling.

Why? Why did it have to be *her*, and why did he have so much rage and pain and sorrow at the sight of her after all this time? Of course, she betrayed him. People always did. The promise of the Hemlock queen's gold and gratitude was too sweet for anyone in Faerieland to resist, even if Nyxara had loved him at first.

Emrys shook the thought away. She never had.

But she had seemed so different at first. Both her and Andreas. They'd been so kind, cooking him breakfast the day after their first romp, exchanging worried looks when he said he planned on partying through every home that side of Faerieland until something stuck for a moment, then offering to let him stay, then offering him a place with them, then saying they loved him.

Andreas had sounded so upset as Emrys listened to Nyxara reveal her plan. Had he really been appalled that his partner was turning on one of their own? Or had he merely needed convincing, and Emrys had acted before that could happen?

Had he died regretting that the plan hadn't worked or in emotional agony because Emrys hadn't believed he was innocent?

Emrys flinched as he swallowed, grateful for the distraction, and gingerly traced the scar along his neck. Nearly dying at the hands of a former lover had gotten him laid, at least. That was a plus. He absently brushed his lips where Zackary had kissed him before allowing Emrys to kiss the stretch of his broad chest as he stroked the hard, hot length of him, leaving Zackary breathless and choking back groans for fear they'd be too loud. He'd come with Emrys' name on his tongue, then gently pushed Emrys on his back before kissing all down his stomach and taking his cock in his mouth.

Between the perfect, burning sensation of his shaft on Zackary's tongue, his head in Zackary's throat, and the sweet, filthy things Zackary whispered between workings—calling him "brat" and "princeling" whenever Emrys whimpered for more—Emrys hadn't lasted long. The orgasm had wracked him so hard that he hardly remembered Zackary crawling back up to the pillows and pulling Emrys close before sleep took them both.

Now here he was, heat building under his skin at the mere memory and wondering if, for the first time in his life, Emrys had made a mistake in getting what he wanted.

He shook the thought away—because how the hell was good sex ever a bad idea?—and got out of bed.

He took another shower, the phantom stick of blood and sand grating against his skin, and made his way down the stairs into the kitchen, where Zackary stood at the stove and Gracie sat at the table, nursing her morning coffee.

Zackary turned and smiled with a spatula in his hand. A golden pancake sizzled in the skillet, speckled with chocolate chips. A tall stack sat on a plate at his side. Morning, sunshine. I was just about to see if you wanted breakfast."

Emrys' hunger tangled into nausea. He swallowed hard, forcing himself to remember how Zackary had done the exact same thing when Maryam had learned she was half-demon. This wasn't tied to the sex. It was just something Zackary did because he was a disgustingly sweet person. It was nothing like what Nyxara and Andreas did for him.

Nothing like that at all.

Zackary's brow furrowed. "Are you okay? Do you need to lie back down?"

Emrys shook his head and took a seat at the table full of fresh fruit, butter, and syrup, as if this morning couldn't get any more horribly wholesome. I'm fine." He poured himself a glass of orange juice. Are chocolate-chip pancakes your answer to everything?"

Of course not," Zackary replied, somewhat indignantly. Sometimes I make waffles. The occasional crepe." He flipped the pancake onto the stack and brought the plate to the table, placing it in the center. "Breakfast is a bit of a love language for me, though."

Gracie motioned to Emrys over the spread. You first."

Emrys squirmed under the attention as he forked a pair of pancakes onto his plate. "Thanks. And thank you for taking such good care of me last night. I appreciate it."

Gracie waved the gratitude away. Please. Zackary did most of the work."

Zackary paused, his forked pancakes hovering between the community plate and his own before he set them down, gaze intently focused on the process of slathering on butter.

Emrys' insides churned with anxiety. He was supposed to be teasing Zackary, making comments about just how good of a job Zackary did taking care of him so Zackary could glare at him and kick him under the table, but he...couldn't.

Fuck. Is this what happened when you slept with someone you cared about? No wonder Emrys hadn't done it in fifty years—It was fucking terrible.

Zackary cleared his throat as he cut his food. "Did you tell the witches we found the killer?"

Gracie took a long sip of coffee before answering. Not yet. I wasn't sure if you wanted to wait until it was good and settled."

I don't see how we can settle it now," Emrys chimed in. We've lost the element of surprise. We're gonna have one hell of a time hunting Nyxara down now that she knows we're after her."

Gracie's eyes bulged and she blinked. You know this woman?"

Emrys scowled, mostly inwardly at himself. We were lovers, once upon a time."

Gracie blinked again, looked as though she might speak, thought better of it, and took another drink of coffee.

"We need to reassess our resources first before going forward." Zackary turned to Emrys. "Starting with you."

Emrys locked his gaze firmly on his plate. "What about me?"

Zackary helped himself to the bacon. That power of yours—what is it? How does it work?"

Emrys took his time chewing, trying to think of a real answer. "I don't know. It's only happened twice before—once when Nyxara tried to kill me like I said last night, and..." Emrys' mouth dried around a bite of food, turning it to paste as he tried to swallow. "The first time was when my mother died. It's tied to fear and danger, somehow."

Zackary snorted. "You infiltrated the Order, unleashed a bunch of demon-possessed people on a room full of exorcists, and then fought off said demon-possessed people. You were in plenty of danger then and you never mentioned this power manifesting."

"You *what*?" Gracie exclaimed. She shook her head before Emrys could answer. "Never mind. Tell me the story later. What was your headspace like when this power woke up? What about that was different from other times you were in danger?"

Emrys paused to think, needing so much brainpower that he couldn't chew and focus the same time as he tried to remember.

Every time those powers manifested, he'd been swept away by a tsunami of sensations and emotions that he'd never stopped to name. His heart raced with the echoes of hurt, betrayal, confusion, and shame that had put a deafening roar in his ears and sweat in his palms. The images were all a blur, his mind racing with the typhoon of feelings that hadn't subsided until he was safe once more, having run like a coward—first through the walls of the Hemlock keep, which had been carved within an enormous elm tree. It had molded into tunnels and turns allowing him to escape the Hemlock queen while she tortured his mother. Then, flames had sprouted from his fingertips as Nyxara tried to bind his wrists, a knife to his throat, saying she'd kill him if he didn't stop pleading to Andreas to help him. He'd burned her, and then he'd burned up the first place he'd called home since his mother's death, running into the night as Andreas screamed for him to come back, trapped in the flames and collapsing beams. Emrys curled in on himself, his chest crumbling inward with its own weight.

Gods, he really was a coward.

"I felt bad."

Zackary frowned, raising an eyebrow. "Care to elaborate?"

"I was hurt, scared, and unimaginably vulnerable." Now that the words had started, Emrys couldn't get them to stop. I need something, *anything,* to get me away from people who wanted me dead, and I had no one to turn to because, in Faerieland, you either have power or you're a plaything for those who do, like my mother was. I couldn't save her when that bitch queen tortured her to death to get to me, and I couldn't die the way she did in Nyxara's grasps—helpless, the victim of someone twice as powerful and thrice as cruel." Emrys glared daggers at Zackary. Is that elaborate enough, Dr. Phil?"

"Emrys." Gracie frowned, her tone that of a schoolteacher scolding a pupil. "He's trying to help."

It's okay, Gracie." Zackary popped another bite of food into his mouth, unsettlingly calm in the face of Emrys' brooding storm. "What blocks you from harnessing it outside of situations like that? Situations when you're in control, to some extent?"

Emrys tensed. "I don't know."

"Are you getting in your own way?"

Emrys' jaw clenched. "Don't be ridiculous."

"It's not ridiculous at all." Zackary raised his coffee to his lips, gaze boring into Emrys as he drank. "Before we left, you said you were scared to come on this mission because you were afraid you weren't strong enough."

"Because I'm not—"

"Wrong." Zackary sat up a little taller, his shoulders back as steel laced his voice. "You're strong as hell, Emrys."

"Zack, stop—"

"You're powerful as any overly ambitious bastard in Faerieland, just like your father, and that scares the hell out of you."

Emrys shot to his feet, his chair screeching across the floor like thunder. He labored to breathe, the kitchen suddenly too hot for him to get a proper breath. You know what? Fuck you, Zack." He glared down at the demon, fury building in his chest with every second he remained poised and collected. Sorry we can't all lean into our inner immortal sun, or whatever Abrahamic bullshit it is that makes you better than the rest of us."

Zackary didn't even twitch at the barb. "I never said I was better than anyone. I just know what I am." He set the mug down and folded his hands in front of his mouth. "So, what are you, Emrys Hemlock?"

Emrys' teeth ground together, every muscle in his body tightening like a steel cord on a bridge ready to snap.

He marched toward the back door, hands clamped into fists. I'm going on a walk." He snatched his jacket from its hook and slammed the door behind him.

The icy crust above the snow gave way in a satisfying crunch as he stomped across the barren white field. It was good to crush something—break something. It didn't quell the raging squall inside him, but it siphoned the pressure, at least a little bit. He eyed the black line of trees in the distance and realized just how stupid he had been to storm out. Where the hell was he supposed to go?

Truth be told, Emrys could go anywhere. He'd gotten what he wanted, at least something close to it. Zackary had finally caved. Emrys could leave. He could just disappear into those trees and never see Zackary again like he'd originally planned. But that would hurt him. It would hurt Maryam and maybe even Alex. For the first time since his mother died, there were people that would miss him. At least, he hoped they would miss him. They acted so much like they cared.

But so had Nyxara and Andreas.

Emrys stopped short, his vision blurring as his eyes burned, hating everything.

Gods damn him. Why did he have to *feel*? It had been so easy sleeping and partying his way through life, numbing himself with one drug or another when the long span of a lonely, meaningless immortal life got to be too much. Then Zackary had shown up, and, as usual, Emrys had thought with the wrong head, only this time, he'd put himself in a nice, safe, cozy, stable little corner like an idiot because he couldn't trust any of it.

And that meant Zackary was right about him.

The screen door slammed, drawing Emrys' attention back to the house.

He watched as Zackary trudged across the snow toward him.

Fucking hell. How were they in the middle of nowhere, yet somehow Emrys couldn't fume and spiral in peace?

Go away, Zack." Emrys' arms folded against the chill.

Zackary came closer. No. I can't let you help finish this job unless you actually face this."

Emrys barked a bitter laugh. "I'm sorry, *let* me? The Order asked *me* first. You're not better than me just because this is your day job."

Zackary sighed. I have never thought I'm better than you, Emrys. Where do you keep getting that impression?"

Emrys snorted. "Oh, I don't know. The last four months of rejection and mind games have made it pretty clear."

Don't you even dare." Zackary's eyes lit up with anger as he jabbed at Emrys. "I told you my terms—if we're going to be together, we're going to be *together*. I will not be a notch in your belt."

"Sorry to inform you, but that ship has sailed with you at the helm."

Emrys regretted the words the second they slapped Zackary in the face, his rage sputtering out and replaced with regret. Why did he have to be an asshole in addition to a coward?

He stuttered, searching for a way to claw back the sentence as Zackary's face flashed through a flood of emotions, settling on an unreadable mask as he knelt in the snow.

"Zack..." Emrys opened and closed his mouth. Zackary, I'm–"

A snowball nailed him in the mouth, shocking his system with cold and the burning sting of impact. Emrys coughed and sputtered, cringing as dirt crunched between his teeth.

"Shit, Em, I'm sorry." Zackary jogged across the field. "I was aiming for your chest or shoulder."

"And that makes it okay?" Emrys shook ice crystals from his coat collar. "What the hell is wrong with you?"

Zackary scoffed. "Funny. I'm wondering the same about you."

Emrys snatched a handful of snow and whipped it, nailing Zackary on the forehead. The demon yelped and swore as he batted the slush away. Emrys laughed once before panic spiked in his chest at the sight of a mischievous smirk on Zackary's face. The demon snatched up more snow. Emrys ran before he could stand up and launch his ammo.

Snowballs fell to the right and left of him as he labored to escape through the snow. One grazed his ear, and he covered his head. "I'm sorry, alright? I shouldn't have said that. It was mean." One nailed him square between his shoulders, shattering in a blooming ache. "Ow! Will you stop?"

"Nope." Another snowball whizzed by Emrys' face. I tried to talk to you about your feelings and your powers, and that didn't work, so now we're doing this the hard way."

Zack, seriously, knock it off! I'm not Maryam or one of your antediluvian underlings!"

"You're right." A snowball hit Emrys square in the ass. You're a Hemlock. Deal with it."

That was the problem with everything, wasn't it? Why his mother was dead. Why most of Faerieland either wanted to bed him or kill him. Why he had these stupid powers that rooted him so deeply to the earth—all of that was because of the stupid horns on his head that tied him to a family and a throne that wanted to crush him.

But they hadn't, and they wouldn't. Maybe that made him stronger than he thought—less of a coward than he thought.

Emrys skidded to a stop and reached into the snow. Zackary wanted to see his powers? Fine.

He shivered as power shot through the snow like lightning. With the swing of his arm, a whip of ice erupted from the ground and tangled itself around Zackary's raised arm, just as he prepared to throw another snowball.

Emrys glared, too angry to savor the wide-eyed shock on Zackary's face. "I. Said. Stop."

Zackary dropped the snowball, a wicked smile spreading across his face as he wrapped the whip around his arm and took hold. "Dance with me, then."

He yanked hard. Emrys let go before Zackary's strength could knock him off-balance and watched the whip dissolve into a puff of falling snow. He snatched another weapon, this time lifting a rapier of ice from the drifts. Zackary's eyes lit up as he summoned his own blade made of solar flares and scalding heat, then charged. Emrys gritted his teeth as he willed the ice to stay together against the burning, parrying Zackary's swings and doing his best to keep distance between them—distance and speed were his allies against Zackary's size and strength.

You need to learn to get on the offensive." Zackary swiped high.

Emrys ducked. "You're like three times bigger than me." He widened the space between them. "This isn't a fight I can win."

"You can. You're short–"

"And you're a dick."

"So, focus on weapons that let you strike from a distance. Start keeping small weapons, blades maybe, within reach that let you strike quickly if you get in an opponent's reach."

Emrys' grip on his ice raper tightened, the cold of the hilt beginning to burn. "I'm not in the mood for this, Zackary."

"Then stop me."

Emrys bared his teeth and charged, dragging his blade through the snow to gather length.

He attacked in a flurry of slashes and jabs. When he aimed low, Zackary dodged high, lifting off the ground and staying aloft. Emrys reached in the snow and summoned another whip, snapping it forward so that it wrapped around Zackary's ankle, and pulled.

The demon dropped, coming down on top of Emrys and sending the faerie tumbling backward into the snow.

The world spun as his head hit frozen ground. All the air left his lungs in a solid *oof*.

Shit." Zackary scrambled to his hands and knees. "You okay? I didn't mean to land that hard."

"I'm fine."

Zackary's worried face came into focus against the gray sky, his brows knit together as his strawberry-blonde waves curtained their faces.

It would be so easy to reach out and touch him—so easy to cup his face and, for the first time in forever, just *be* with someone, their rushing blood staving off the cold for one another.

Emrys kneed Zackary in the crotch instead.

Zackary yelped in pain and rolled into the snow, one hand over his crushed groin. "What the fuck is wrong with you?" he groaned.

"You said to strike quick if my opponent was close."

"I suppose I did."

The two fell into silence as their breath slowed. Emrys breathed deep the smokey smell of winter as Zackary let both his arms flop out wide, his left fingers brushing Emrys' right.

A crow squawked somewhere in the woods. An owl hooted back a descant to the hushed roar of the wind. Lying like this, the cold so fierce it bit past his clothes and the sky beginning to spill fat snowflakes from the clouds, Emrys almost felt as if didn't have to ever think again. Gods, it would be nice not to think anymore.

But Zackary had to ruin it like he seemed compelled to ruin everything today.

I don't actually hate Valentine's Day," he muttered.

Emrys blinked and turned to look at Zackary. "What?"

Zackary continued to stare at the sky, his gaze distant. "Back at Ectoplasm, I said I hated Valentine's Day. I don't." He took a deep breath. I only get to share it with Maryam. *That's* what I hate. I bitch about it every year, but we always get each other little gifts that make us laugh if nothing else. I don't get to do that for anyone from my first life."

"Oh." The word was small and stupid, tangled in Emrys' confusion and inability to understand loss like that. His mother has never been one for holidays. If anything, holidays meant she was busier than ever in the keep kitchens with little time for him. "Why are you telling me this?"

Zackary shrugged, making the snow crunch. "I may have been a bit heavy-handed in how I handled this situation. It was wrong of me to try and force you into being vulnerable without warning like that. Thought I should offer a bit of myself in return." He turned to Emrys with an eyebrow raised. That seems to be the only way we ever get anywhere."

Emrys turned back to the sky and took a deep breath, allowing the exhale to sink him deeper into the snow. "I don't actually understand anything about my powers. They're not run-of-the-mill magic, I know that much, but that's it. That's all I've ever cared to know." He pictured his mother and her small magic—the way she'd crust violets in sugar with a wave of her hand, the way she'd infuse herbs with comfort and peace so that the bread they were baked into would leave you feeling safe and cared for.

He clenched his hands into fists as grief gripped his heart. *If I use this power, if I understand it, does that make me more of a Hemlock and less of my mother's son? It didn't come from her, so it must have come from the king, and I've never wanted a single thing from that bastard. I'd saw my damn horns off if it got rid of it all. I tried once—the notch healed over in a week.*"

Emrys could practically hear Zackary tense where he lay in the snow. "You've tried to saw off your horns?"

When I was ten. It doesn't hurt *per se, but it does feel like scratching your bones against a chalkboard. The feeling startled me so much that my hand slipped, and I cut myself.*" Emrys lifted his right hand and willed away his glamour to point at a faint scar against his green skin where his lifeline should have been. *Right there. You'd have thought I was dying, the way mother carried on.*" He studied the scar, flexing his hand to shake the cold from his joints. "She made me promise never to try that again." He turned his hand to study the back against the sky, studying the slender fingers and the delicate nail beds his mother loved to say had been her mother's and her mother's before her. "I wish I hadn't listened. These horns got her killed."

He let his hand fall to his side, his fingers brushing Zackary's.

I like your horns," Zackary said. "They make you look dignified. Gods know you need all the extra dignity you can get."

Emrys took a handful of snow and lazily tossed it in Zackary's direction.

The demon chuckled as he dodged the flurry. He settled again, letting his fingers settle between Emrys'.

Emrys shivered. His stomach clenched as he realized it wasn't from the cold.

Emrys..." Zackary paused. "About last night..."

Wheels crunched through frozen slush in Gracie's driveway, giving Emrys an easy excuse to sit up and avoid Zackary's gaze. He watched as a beat-up Jeep skidded to a stop in the muddy slush. Jupiter jumped from the driver's seat in nothing but a T-shirt and ripped jeans as she ran across the front lawn, her makeup smeared and face red.

Emrys scrambled to his feet and took off to meet her, Zackary close behind.

Miss Gracie!" Jupiter tripped, nearly face-planting as she stumbled up the stairs and banged on the door. "Miss Gracie, help!"

Emrys rounded the porch, nearly slipping and landing in the snow as he tried to slow and turn. "What is it?" He bound up the stairs. "What's happened?"

Gracie opened the door, eyes wide at the sight of both Jupiter and Emrys.

It's Stone. He's gone." Jupiter choked down a sob, struggling to get enough air for words. We think the siren took him."

Gracie ushered Jupiter into the living room, one arm around her shoulders as she eased her onto the sofa and handed her a box of tissues.

Zackary excused himself to the kitchen and returned with a glass of water, all of his vulnerability replaced with the stable, in-control mask Emrys hadn't seen since they faced down Peter's demon. The eerie similarity of the pressure in the room sent a chill down Emrys' spine as he leaned against the mantle above the fireplace as Zackary gave Jupiter the water.

"Jupiter, we're gonna need you to take deep breaths and tell us what happened." Zackary eased himself down on Jupiter's other side, placing a hand gingerly on her back.

The witch didn't seem to mind. She gulped down the water, not so much as breathing until the cup was drained. She placed it on a coaster on the table and took another handful of tissues from the box, whipping at her ruined makeup. "His mom called me early this morning. He was supposed to open at the coffee shop where he works, but he didn't show. He wasn't there when she woke up for work, but she didn't think anything of it because he's usually really quiet when he leaves, but he's not answering anyone's calls or text messages."

Dread settled in the pit of Emrys' stomach, threatening to make him sick. "Where's Sammy?"

"She's with Stone's mom at the police station, trying to file a missing person's report."

Gracie frowned. "I don't imagine they'll take it if it's been less than twenty-four hours."

"We don't have the additional twelve hours to wait for that," Zackary chimed in.

"Did you check the beach for him?" Emrys asked.

Jupiter nodded. "We did. Nothing, which gives me a bit of hope that he's still alive."

"It's something." Emrys stood away from the mantle. "Zack, grab the keys. We gotta move."

Jupiter jumped to her feet. "Let me come. You were right yesterday—I'm a terrible coven leader. I share the blame for this. Let me help fix it." Emrys opened his mouth, but she continued. "I can be a decoy. Show me a spell to summon her, and I'll offer myself in Stone's place. Sammy, too."

Emrys turned to Zackary, desperate for guidance one way or another on what to do. He didn't know shit about leadership, about making decisions like this. Zackary was the one who called all the shots in their little band of rejects back home.

The demon studied Emrys for a moment, as if watching the thoughts play across his face, then sighed. "That's essentially the plan we used to take down Anzuri, and he was a Duke of Hell. Nyxara seems just as cocky, if not more so. It's worth a shot."

Emrys let out a bitter laugh. "Oh, trust me, she's plenty cockier than a Duke of Hell." He bit at his thumbnail as he tried to think. "The trickier part is going to be getting her out with a spell cast during the day, now that the full moon is behind us." He traced his memory, every spell, incantation, and charm he'd ever seen or performed, and came up empty.

At least, empty when it came to spells made of small magics.

"I'm going to have to write a spell from scratch." His gaze shifted to Gracie. "Do you have any paper I can use? And an empty jar?"

Gracie got to her feet, darted into the study, and returned with a spiral notebook and a pen. "No jars. I used the last of them for apple butter this fall."

Emrys took the items and wrestled them into his coat pocket. "That's fine. And thank you." He motioned to Jupiter. "I need you to get something with Stone's essence—hair from a brush, dirty clothes, something like that. Meet us at the pizza place from yesterday. Is the metaphysical shop open today?"

Jupiter nodded. "Yeah—someone's covering my shift."

Emrys pointed to Zackary and headed for the door. "C'mon. We're going to need more pagan trappings."

Zackary grabbed his keys and wallet, scrambling to follow Emrys out the door with Jupiter on his heels.

And Gracie.

Emrys did a double take at the sight of the woman reaching for the back door of the rental. "Gracie, respectfully, what the hell are you doing?"

"There are paths not on the map." She shut the door and buckled her seatbelt. "Paths leading to more remote beaches and caves that we don't like sharing with tourists. They're going to be your best bet for finding Stone and dealing with the siren away from the water, but they're going to be hard to find in the snow. We don't have time for you to bumble around in the forest."

Emrys looked over the top of the car at Zackary, desperate for guidance that would result in Gracie staying home and safe.

Instead, Zackary let out an exasperated sigh as he slid into the driver's seat and started the engine. "Just get in the car. We don't have time to fight about this."

Emrys obeyed, slightly flabbergasted. "You're seriously going to let her come?"

Zackary peeled out of the muddy driveway and onto the road. "She used to be part of the Order. How well do you think telling her no is really going to work?"

Emrys silently conceded that Zackary was right, but as he watched Gracie in the rearview mirror, her green eyes alight with a familiar fire, Emrys realized that her association with the Order wasn't likely the only reason she wouldn't take no for an answer. He reminded her of someone...

He shook the thoughts away and began to scribble in Old Fae on the pad of paper.

No sooner had Zackary put the car in park did Emrys jump out, jogging up the sidewalk and into the store, the Order's credit card in his hand. Zackary nervously tapped along to the radio against the steering wheel, desperate for a distraction. He eyed Gracie in the rearview, who had apparently had time to grab a knitting project on her way out the door.

Zackary smiled as he watched the needles weave together a panel of deep purple fabric. "You can craft at a time like this?"

Gracie scowled down at her project. "I'll go stir crazy if I don't."

Zackary chuckled. "Fair enough." He tapped against the steering wheel again. "Where's this trail you mentioned?"

Gracie spared Zackary a glance as she adjusted the ball of yarn at her side. "It's a branch off Sparrow trail. Nearly impossible to find in the snow if you don't know what to look for. It leads to a clearing locals like to use when they need to get away from town—teenage parties, seasonal religious rituals, things like that. It's inland, so the siren won't have easy access to the water, either for escape or for a weapon. We don't need anyone else's throat cut this weekend."

Zackary shivered. "No shit." He watched Gracie continue to knit, her face scrunched as she fastened off the end of one row and started another, one eyebrow slightly raised, and her mouth squished to one side as she worked. Dread settled in Zackary's veins like a sludge as he realized why Gracie looked so familiar.

Maryam made that exact same face when she was working a particularly tricky crochet pattern. Sarah made it when she was reading a particularly dense piece of theological writing.

Zackary's grip tightened on the steering wheel as he tried to swallow the words lodged in the back of his throat. This wasn't the time to ask—hell, there *wasn't* a time to ask, but the words escaped before he could stop them.

"How well did you know Father Claude, Gracie?"

The rhythmic clicking of knitting needles continued. "Quite well. By the end of the first year of school, we were practically inseparable."

"Were you ever more than friends?"

Gracie scoffed. "He was already an ordained Catholic priest by the time I met him."

"That's not what I asked."

The needles went silent. Zackary dared to glance at the rearview to find a dark, calculating look on her face, telling him all he needed to know.

His goddaughter had the same exact expression in her arsenal. So did her aunt.

The passenger door popped open, making him jump as Emrys slid in, a paper bag dangling from his wrist. "Okay, we're set." He set the bag between his feet on the floor. "Let's go meet the girls."

Gracie dug her phone from her pocket, the shadow now gone from her face. "Jupiter just texted me. They're there."

"Perfect." Emrys clapped his hands at Zackary. "Let's go. Chop, chop."

Zackary scowled as he put the car in reverse. "Being obnoxious isn't helping matters."

Emrys settled into his seat and went back to scribbling his spell. "No, but it makes me feel better."

Zackary pulled onto the road toward the pizza place and glanced in the mirror at Gracie calmly knitting as if nothing had happened—as if he hadn't nearly shattered the peace she had built or the unanswered questions no one back home had dared to ask." Maybe they shouldn't. Maybe it was better this way.

And maybe, like Emrys' issues with Nyxara, the only way to really heal a wound was to take off the old, dirty bandage and do the hard, painful work of sewing it up.

But just like Emry's old relationship, Gracie's relationship to the Order and the people within it wasn't Zackary's injury to treat.

The ragtag team left the rental car at the pizza place and piled into Jupiter's Jeep. She insisted that it had bested multiple Lake Superior winters and had better snow tires than the rental. When Zackary turned to Emrys for his thoughts on the matter (as if he were *responsible* and *smart* or something), he didn't argue. He only suggested that Gracie sit up front since she was giving directions, despite the fact that Zackary's knees practically reached his chin as he, Emrys, and Sammy piled into the back.

Thirty minutes out of town, Gracie led them off the road. Emrys decided he had made the right call as the Jeep jolted and jumped as deep, virgin snow crunched and packed beneath the wheels. Twenty minutes later (most of which Emrys spent worried they'd get stuck) Gracie told Jupiter to stop and the others to pile out.

The snow reached nearly halfway up Emrys' shins, making every step into the woods a chore. By the time they reached a small, untouched clearing, sweat trickled from his nape down his spine, making him shiver.

Jupiter panted, gloved hands on her hips as she tried to catch her breath. "What now?"

"Help me pack down the snow into a circle for the ritual." Emrys gestured to Zackary. "Set up a glamoured parameter. Gracie, can you keep a lookout?"

She nodded as the others got to work.

With the snow packed down, Emrys laid out a candle and crystals in a pattern nearly identical to the one he made the night before, with the addition of a blanket for the girls to sit on. Once he dried kindling the best he could, pulling moisture from twigs and branches, letting it fall to the snow like mist, he tasked Zackary with building a fire as he handed Jupiter the spell.

She recoiled, trying to shove the paper back into his hand. "You should be the one to do it."

Emrys shook his head and gently took Jupiter's wrist, curling her fingers around the paper. "Nyxara will be expecting someone super-natural. She won't be threatened by you. She's so damn full of herself that she'll probably be curious about what you're willing to trade for Stone." He squeezed Jupiter's hand as her brow furrowed. "You're a witch. You're a *coven leader*. You can do this, Jupiter."

She studied Emrys' face, then took a deep breath, letting it out in a giant puff. "Yes. Okay. I can do this."

Emrys smiled and patted her hand. "That's my girl." He dug a small glass vial from his bag and a small bone-handled knife. He approached the arch of kindling Zackary had built and kneeled, placing the bottle on the snow and the knife on his palm, right along the faint scar on his lifeline.

"You were only partially right earlier, Zack," he said.

Emrys could practically hear one eyebrow raise as Zackary asked, "About?"

"What I'm afraid of." The blade sliced into Emrys' hand. He winced at the cut but refused to look away. "It's not strength I'm afraid of. It's power." He dropped the knife and lifted the bottle, letting his dripping blood dye the sides deep ruby red as it pooled. "I may have their name and their magic, but I never want to be a Hemlock. I've seen what being one does to your soul."

Zackary folded his arms, head slightly to the side. "I think being a Hemlock means whatever the hell you want it to mean." He shrugged. "But I can't make that decision for you—that's your path to decide."

Emrys silently placed the bottle within the kindling, careful not to collapse the structure as he dug a book of matches from his pocket and lit the handful of dry leaves he could find. He reached his bleeding hand toward the pitiful flames, willing it to burn hotter, willing a small breeze to blow so the wood would catch. Once he was confident it would keep burning, he wiped his bloody hand against the snow, the wound already healing thanks to his faerie blood, and faced the others. "Jupiter, Sammy, you're on summoning duty. Jupiter, give Gracie your keys. I want her in the car, engine on, ready to leave the second you two grab Stone."

The three mortals nodded, exchanging the car keys before making their way to their positions.

Emrys turned to Zackary as the two witches settled down. "Get a high vantage point along there somewhere." He motioned to the tree line behind the girls. "I'll take the opposite side."

Zackary nodded. As Emrys turned to take his post, he called out, "Emrys?"

Emrys turned, watching Zackary calculate and fight with himself. His heart hammered in his chest, desperate for Zackary to hurry and say something—something maybe with a certain "L" word.

"Be smart. Be safe."

Emrys' heart sank a bit, but he nodded all the same. "You too."

Without another word, he crossed the clearing to a tree with a low foothold. Emrys turned back and kneeled, his hand sinking into the snow, already numb from the cold. He silently ordered the snow to shift like sand, hiding the groups' footprints, leaving the ritual circle as the only sign of disturbance.

With that, he scaled the tree, selected his perch, and peered through the branches, willing a bow and arrow to form from the bark, a string of sap and pulp pulled tight, the tip of the arrow aimed just past the fire.

And then, he waited.

Jupiter's voice reached him on the wind, low and forceful with magical intention. Sammy's voice joined her, higher and feather light with its soprano tone. Energy skittered along Emrys' skin as power crept from beneath the snow, swirling and blowing like a living thing as Nyxara was summoned, *forced* by the power of Emrys' Hemlock blood that burned in that fire. He squinted and then blinked against the icy wind.

And then, there she was, standing before the witches like a dark goddess summoned for a sabbath.

The girls scrambled to their feet and huddled together, cowering as Nyxara towered over them.

She lifted her head, watching the girls through her wet hair, dark eyes narrowed, and mouth twisted in a sinister smile. "Brave little witches, summoning me directly." She tilted her head to the side. "Brave, or very, very stupid." Her gaze flickered down to the fire, then back to the girls. "And with Hemlock blood." She gave a huff of laughter. "Tell me, sisters, where is Emrys? What did that coward promise you in exchange for doing his dirty work?"

"Give us back Stone, and I'll *think* about telling you what Emrys asked for," Jupiter fired back.

Emrys smirked. Quick thinking. Maybe he liked that witch after all.

Nyxara tittered. "Oh, sweet child. I'm afraid that's not how this is going to go." A hand of glass-like ice rose in place of the one Zackary had severed. Nyxara gave it a dainty flick, as if it had always been a part of her, and a pillar of flurrying snow rose from the ground, falling away to reveal Stone's limp body encased in ice with only his drenched, pale head exposed, his lips already a frightening shade of blue. Nyxara flexed her hand, and Stone weakly whimpered as the ice squeezed in on him.

Nyxara beamed, her smile bloodthirsty as the girls called for her to stop. "Make Emrys deliver himself to me, and I'll *think* about not crushing your friend to death."

Emrys held his breath and took in every little detail of Nyxara—the way she refused to blink, the subtle small smile across her thin lips, and the gloating, bloodthirsty light in her eyes. He knew that look all too well. It meant that she wasn't bluffing.

He let his arrow fly, aiming just to her left so that the wood whizzed by her head, slicing through a lock of wet hair before landing in the snow.

Nyxara only laughed, her head back and her sharp teeth visible, unfazed by the gesture. "Oh, Emrys," she called. "No need to be such a sore loser."

"This isn't about me losing." Emrys tossed the bow and arrow to the ground, then leaped down after them. He landed on the balls of his feet, then stood tall as he glared the siren down. "I just never want to miss a chance to show how much I fucking hate you."

Nyxara dismissively clicked her tongue and shook her head. "So petty. I thought you would have grown up a bit in the last fifty years."

Emrys began to cross the snow, his gaze locked on her. "Cut the bullshit and tell me what you want before Stone freezes to death and you lose your bargaining chip."

Nyxara dropped her hand to her hip. "Oh, he won't. Don't worry." She looked Stone's frozen body up and down. "He's far from comfortable in there, but I know how cold I can let mortals get before the fun's over. And I want from you what I've always wanted, lover." She turned back to Emrys, her eyes alight with hungry fire. "I want to serve your head to the Hemlock queen on a spike in exchange for gold and favor."

Rage turned Emrys' blood molten as those words reverberated through his skull.

I want from you what I've always wanted.

What I've always wanted.

Always.

The realization must have read on Emrys' face, because Nyxara laughed again, the sound bitter and condescending. "Oh, don't look so angry, Emrys. Surely, deep down, you must have known." Her eyes narrowed. "What else could anyone ever really want from someone like you? People get bored of their favorite whores all the time—"

"You're trying to get under my skin so that I lash out again," Emrys snapped. "It won't work. I'm not the smartest bastard in Faerieland, but I can learn on occasion." He glanced toward Stone, then the girls from the corner of his eye. "But I also recognize when I'm beat."

He stepped between Nyxara and the witches, slowly kneeling, his hands remaining where the siren could see them, and placed one hand on the packed snow. He took deep breaths, exhaling both air and energy, sending it coursing through the snow until they formed a sheer-white broadsword of snow and ice. Emrys got to his feet, lifting the blade with him, struggling to look sure of himself under the weight.

"Free Stone, and you'll have my head." He held the sword out toward Nyxara.

The siren narrowed her eyes into a sharp glare, searching Emrys' faith for a sliver of untruth. "What are you playing at?"

"I'm not playing at anything," Emrys said. "I've lost. I try to touch you, and you'll crush Stone, so I'm surrendering."

"I don't believe you."

Emrys rolled his eyes and tossed the sword. Nyxara scrambled to catch the hilt, nearly losing her balance as the blade hit the snow.

"I'm handing you my death." Emrys folded his arms. "What more proof do you need?"

A smirk brushed Nyxara's lips. "You're really giving up so easily?"

"You said it yourself." Emrys dropped his gaze, his grip tight on his upper arms. "I have nothing else to offer than what you see before you. I might as well use it for good for once."

The witches whispered and hissed behind him before Jupiter finally called out, "Emrys, you can't do this!"

Emrys whirled and glared in a silent order to hush. As he turned back to face Nyxara, he spied a flash of movement in the trees behind her, just as he had hoped he would.

He forced the smirk from his face and glared at the siren. "Let Stone go or I'll run. You know how good I am at it. You'll never get a shot like this again."

She glared back with a growl. "Fine. It's not as satisfying as I would have liked, but the Hemlock queen will pay handsomely either way, I suppose."

With a wave of her hand, the ice encasing Stone shattered, freeing the boy to collapse into the snow.

Emrys shot out a hand before the witches could run for him. "Wait!" He stared down Nyxara. "They get beyond the trees, or there's no deal."

Nyxara gave an annoyed huff, then gave the witches a dismissive shooing motion. "Take him and go. I ever sense magic from any of you three again, and I'll kill you on the spot."

The witches didn't argue. They didn't even look Nyxara's way. They only gathered up their friend, one arm over each set of shoulders, and awkwardly walked across the field back toward Jupiter's car. Emrys watched from the corner of his eye. Once they disappeared into the trees, he lowered himself to his knees, arms out with his palms up in surrender.

Nyxara took a step forward, raising the sword as best she could with a grunt. "You had to find a way to be a pain in the ass until the very end, didn't you?"

"Of course." Emrys kept his gaze forward, scanning the woods for any sign of Zackary. "Because fuck you."

Nyxara scoffed as she poised to swing. "Any more final words?"

"Um...Fuck you in *particular*?"

Nyxara dropped the blade.

A flash of light shot from the woods.

Emrys dropped. The sword grazed the top of his horns as Nyxara struggled to redirect the blade, an enraged cry splitting the air. Emrys launched himself at Nyxara's gut, his horns making contact with her diaphragm and drawing a satisfying wheeze from her lungs. Emrys did his best to fight back the swell of pride as he wrestled Nyxara's arms to her side. He had kept his promise—Nyxara had received his head, but Emrys hadn't specified how she'd receive it.

The siren screeched and thrashed, her nails raking across Emrys' face as she summoned a wave of snow to knock him off. Emys choked and sputtered as he fought his way from the powder, a pair of strong hands finally pulling him completely free. He wiped the slush from his eyes as Zackary placed him on his feet.

"Are you alright?"

"I'm fine," Emrys said through a cough, pushing past him as Nyxara disappeared into the woods. "Don't let her get away."

Zackary followed suit, overtaking Emrys as they sprinted across the field. "That was wildly stupid of you. What if I hadn't moved in time?"

Emrys did his best to shrug as he ran, his lungs burning. "I knew you wouldn't let me die. You think I'm too pretty."

Zackary rolled his eyes.

Emrys spied a rip in the arm of Zackary's coat, soaked dark with blood. "You flew right into that bitch's sword, so I don't want to hear it."

"You *gave* her the damn sword—"

A sharp tendril of snow shot from the underbrush as they crossed into the trees, nearly skewering Zackary through the neck before Emrys shoved him aside. He dove behind a tree for cover, Zackary hiding behind another, both panting and listening for Nyxara's movements.

Red tinted Emrys' vision as he caught his breath, and the last few seconds played back in his mind.

She'd almost killed Zackary. *Zackary,* who had a goddaughter waiting at home and souls to save and other demons to redeem.

Energy crackled at Emrys' fingertips as rage skittered over his skin like static.

A spike of ice whizzed by his head, slicing through the bark. Emrys dove for different cover, launching a shower of ice shards of his own before landing behind a thick birch.

Nyxara cackled somewhere nearby. "You think you're *somebody* now because someone worth a damn is fucking you?" she called. "You think that changes *anything*?"

Emrys huffed a bitter chuckle. "Jealous much?" He paused, listening for signs of an approach. "If you weren't such a crazy, power-hungry bitch, you might know what it's like to be wanted again."

Nyxara scoffed. "Oh, please. You think that demon *wants* you? He knows what you are, just like I did—a little whiny pawn who will do *anything* to feel like somebody loves him. To feel like he *matters* to someone."

Emrys did his best to block out the words and listen to where they were coming from. If he closed his eyes, he could picture her behind him to the left. Low to the ground. Emrys braced himself, then dared to come out from hiding long enough to launch barbs of ice and sleet at a low bushel of juniper that gave way, making Nyxara shriek in anger and pain as the barbs found their mark. She jumped from her cover, launching a whip of snow at Emrys' throat. He dropped and rolled behind a fallen tree. The attack shot over his head. Emrys reached out and froze it solid, rolling out of the way of the newly formed hunk of ice.

"Give me a little credit," Emrys panted. "I drew a boundary eventually. It's not my fault you didn't like it."

Nyxara gave a tired huff of laughter. "You know, if you had just shut up and been a good little doll, I would have kept you around a bit longer. But you just couldn't play nice, so it was time to trade you in."

Emrys' stomach rolled with disgust at the memories. The way he'd let Nyxara hurt him, the way he'd let her make him bleed, all to feel like he might be loved. "Jesus Christ, why are you such a sadistic cunt?"

"I'm a siren." Nyxara laughed as she spoke, her voice closer than Emrys would have liked. "I play, I fuck, and I kill—usually in some combination of the three. It's the natural order of things." Her voice came from directly over his head.

He snapped his gaze upward to see her towering over him, her sharp teeth in a triumphant smile.

Emrys bolted. Snow snaked around his neck, lifting him to his feet and cutting off his air. It whipped him around so fast that the world spun, and pain shot down his neck, red-hot and pulsing.

"*Your* place in that order is on your back, on your knees, or earning someone a hell of a lot of gold with those pretty horns of yours." Nyxara closed her hand into a fist, bloodthirsty glee lighting up her eyes as black dots danced in Emrys' vision and his vision began to blur. "Lucky for me, it's going to be my pocket."

Zackary dropped from the trees behind her, a blur of movement, his own blade lifted as Nyxara whirled on him, summoning a spear of ice, aiming for Zackary's chest.

Emrys' blood gave one final rush in desperation, drawing a pillar of ice from the ground at his feet, sending it straight through Nyxara's heart.

Time stopped. Her magic disintegrated, dropping Emrys to the ground. Zackary was there to catch him, holding him as he gasped and coughed, blinking the world back to normal as his own magic dissolved and Nyxara collapsed to the ground, a rod of ice still jutting through her chest.

Zackary took Emrys' face in his hand, turning his head away from Nyxara's crumpled form. "Em, look at me." His gaze darted across Emrys' features, eyes wide with panic. "Em, say something."

"I'm fine," Emrys rasped, wiggling out of Zackary's grip. "Definitely not into choking anymore, but I'm fine."

Zackary sighed, his shoulders slumping and his face crumpled in a mix of disappointment and relief. "Really? Did we need a joke right now?"

"You might not have needed it, but I definitely did."

Nyxara coughed, cutting Emrys' relief short. He watched in horror as she struggled to her hands and knees.

Emrys pulled away from Zackary, stepping over the fallen tree toward her.

The demon reached out and grabbed him by the arm. "Em, don't."

Emrys pulled away, staring down at Nyxara as she tried to crawl away, his mind an eerie ocean of calm at the sight.

"Emrys—"

"I got it."

"She's neutralized. You don't have to—"

Emrys turned and glared daggers. "I said I got it."

"Do what you're told, Emrys." Nyxara laughed as her throat filled with blood. "You don't want your demon beau coming for your head, too, do you? I don't think you'd be quite so lucky in a fight where you can't hide behind him."

Red tinted Emrys' vision. He snatched a hold of the ice and yanked, making Nyxara screech as he pulled it free, her blood dying the ice red.

"Emrys!"

Emrys whirled on Zackary with a snarl. "Stay the *fuck* out of this, Zackary."

"Look at you, talking back like a big boy. Andreas would be proud."

Energy shivered through the ice, twisting and morphing the rod into an ax with a wide, slender curved blade. "Don't you *dare* talk to me about Andreas."

Nyxara looked up at Emrys through her hair, her eyes wide and crazed as she yelled, "I'll speak however I like of him! He was mine before you came along and poisoned him!" She coughed and hacked, speckling the snow with blood.

A dark, satisfied smirk tugged at Emrys' lips.

Nyxara took a wheezing breath. "He truly came to love you in the end, you know."

Emrys' blood went cold as Nyxara's expression eased.

"He tried to reason with me when I told him the truth."

Emrys' grip tightened on the ax. "Stop it."

"He said if I ever talked about turning you in again, he'd take you and leave me."

He was too frozen to use the ax. His mind was too loud with roaring blood and distant screams. He could hardly even see straight. "I said stop!"

"He loved you, and you burned him alive."

"STOP IT!"

"You murdered the only person who ever truly wanted you."

"SHUT UP!"

Spikes of ice shot from the ground, impaling the siren, suspending her off the ground, like a marionette held in the air by her strings. Emrys went blank, his brain nothing but white noise as Nyxara gurgled, rasped, and finally went limp.

Had...had he done that? He must have, but he didn't even remember touching his power. It had just...happened.

Before he could decide, Nyxara's body faded into translucence, shattering into a spray of dark, clear, and ruby ice among the bed of spikes, like she had never existed at all.

Just like Andreas after Emrys' fire burned him alive.

One second Emrys was rooted to the snow, the next he was hurling. His eyes squeezed shut with the violence of it as if his guts were trying to escape him. He didn't blame them—he wanted to escape him too. Instead, he had to hold on as his stomach wrenched until there was nothing left, leaving him shaky and lightheaded as he spit bile on the snow and wiped his mouth.

A warm hand settled on Emrys' back.

"Emrys..."

He scrambled away, turning on Zackary with a glare. "Get off me."

Zackary held his hands up, his body curled small as if he was approaching a fawn. "Emrys, it's okay. I've got you. It's—"

"HOW IS ANY OF THIS OKAY?" Emrys screamed back.

Zackary didn't answer. He only watched Emrys with pained, gentle eyes.

Emrys couldn't stand it. Not the gentleness. Not the comfort. Not his own overwhelming fear of Zackary knowing the full truth, knowing he couldn't escape the ash, death, and destruction that came with the blood he hadn't asked for, the acts he feared had been forced on his mother. He was a broken bastard of a thing. Nothing about him was right.

Worst of all, he knew Zackary wouldn't care, just like his mother and Andreas hadn't cared, which was why they were as dead as Nyxara.

"Don't you get it?" Emrys motioned to the shards of ice that had once been someone he had dared to love, and the magic, *his* magic, that had killed her. "You can't love this shit-show away. You can't love me into some safe, tame, proper, clean little lamb to make yourself feel better about wanting to fuck me."

Zackary's breaking heart played on his face in real-time. "That's not what I'm trying to do. That's *never* what I've want to do. I..." His jaw clenched as he swallowed hard. I want to be with you for *you*, Emrys."

A bitter, tired laugh escaped Emrys' lips. Why did Zackary have to be so goddamn good? Why did he have to make this so fucking hard? "Let me put it in terms you'll understand." He met the demon's pained gaze. "We will *never* be together the way you want. I flirt, I play games, and I fuck, usually in some combination of the three. Save all this effort and pinning for the shitty god you want to crawl back to so much. You might have better luck."

Zackary stared as if he'd been slapped, then melted into an expression of carefully curated neutrally, all the light and kindness that Emrys loved fading away.

Emrys' stomach dropped to his feet. No, no, no, he had gone too far. He hadn't meant to be so mean, but what else could he do to keep Zackary from believing that they could be something good? Something special?

Because as long as Emrys was neither of those things, they never could be.

"Thanks for clearing that up for me, Em." Zackary folded his arms, his body rigid and his gaze cold. "I'm going to go check on the others. Stone might need medical attention."

Emrys choked down the lump in his throat. "You...you do that. I'll take down the glamours."

Zackary nodded, turned, and walked away.

Emrys watched him go, waiting until he had crossed the clearing before dropping to his hands and knees, letting the heat of his tears melt the snow.

Emrys did as he said. He took down the glamours. And then he walked.

And walked.

And walked.

He didn't know where he was going, he just knew he couldn't stop, or his own brain would swallow him whole. He considered letting it—considered sitting down and seeing what would happen if he cried himself to sleep in the snow and let the drifts take him, making him part of the landscape, but he couldn't.

Maryam would worry. Alex might worry.

Despite everything, even Zackary would worry—he was too kind and good not to.

Still, as night fell, Emrys couldn't bring himself to return to Gracie's house. Not yet. He needed more time.

To do what, he couldn't say. Whatever it was, he needed to do it in town, where he would at least have some cover from the biting wind.

The cold brick and siding of the buildings helped less than he had hoped. By the time the stars were out in full, Emrys couldn't feel a single inch of himself anymore.

But then he walked past the metaphysical store, locked up and abandoned for the night.

Emrys didn't consider it breaking and entering—not when he didn't break anything, and he fully planned on leaving a gift of some sort—some small proof of a faerie's favor to lend to the store's credibility.

In the corner of the store sat a fort made of shawls and blankets with a sign that read "Tarot Readings." Inside was a small round coffee table and enough cushions and pillows that Emrys fell asleep the second he arranged them faintly into the shape of a bed and plopped face-first on top of them.

No sooner had he fallen into a dead sleep did someone wake him with the exclamation of, "Jesus Bleeding Christ! E-...Emrys?"

He blinked against the bright fluorescent lights and squinted to find Jupiter at the fort entrance. "What are you doing here?" he grumbled, shielding his eyes.

Jupiter stuttered around an answer for a moment. "What am I—I *work* here. What are *you* doing here? And how did you get in without tripping the alarms?"

"Magic." Emrys sat up and rubbed his eyes, then dug his phone from his pocket to find it dead. "What time is it?"

"About six. I came in early to do a tarot reading stream." Jupiter's shock shifted into concern. "Are you okay? You kinda..." She scanned Emrys over. "You kinda look like shit."

Emrys snorted. "I feel like shit, so that makes sense. How's Stone?"

"He had the early stages of hypothermia, but the doctor ruled that it wasn't bad enough to take him to the hospital in Marquette. He's staying at the clinic for a few days so they can keep an eye on him."

"Good." Emrys nodded, moving to crawl out of the fort. "Good. If there's nothing else, I'll get out of your hair."

"Wait." Jupiter moved to block his path. "Do you want to...talk or something?"

Emrys raised a brow.

"Zackary came to the car without you, and we started to worry. He said you were fine, but he seemed off. Did you two fight or something?"

Emrys leaned back and massaged his temple. "I really don't feel like talking, Jupiter."

She grinned. "I have just the thing for that."

She disappeared from the entrance. Too tired to make a break for it, Emrys flopped back into his makeshift bed and closed his eyes. Maybe he could at least get a few more minutes of sleep.

Instead, he got Jupiter's company, and a steaming mug placed in front of him.

He sat up with a groan and pulled it towards him, savoring the warm smell of vanilla and spices. He took a sip to find a bite of whiskey intertwined with dark roast coffee. He drank deep, then gave Jupiter a tired smile as she sat across from him. "You're right. This is just the thing."

Jupiter smiled, her eyes lighter. "It usually is. So, have at it. Spill."

Emrys sighed, then gave Jupiter a wry smirk. "Buckle up," he said. "Because this is one hell of a ride."

Jupiter left and came back with the entire bottle of booze a third of the way through Emrys' tale, so "one hell of a story" might have been an understatement. Still, it felt good to let it all out, no matter how nasty it was. Jupiter was a good listener, nodding along and giving a little "mm-hm" at all the right parts without a single glimpse of judgment on her face. When he was finished, Emrys sat back, poured himself more whiskey, and waited for her to process it all.

"That is..."

Emrys grimaced against the burn of cheap alcohol. "Yep."

"Wow."

"I know. That's why I warned you."

Jupiter stared down at the table, then took the bottle and poured herself a shot, which she immediately threw back. After her own grimace passed, she studied Emrys in silence for a moment.

"Question." Jupiter said the word slowly, as if unsure how to finish the rest of her thought. "Did you just want to spill your guts, or are you open to advice?"

Emrys gave a wild wave for her to go on and took another sip of whiskey.

"Have you considered trying to be Zack's friend instead of a total thot?"

Emrys choked and sputtered, spilling his drink down the front of his coat. "Sorry," he wheezed, "but I think I've made sure that friendship is off the table."

"See, there's this thing called an apology—"

"Never heard of it."

"And this other thing called therapy."

"Faeries don't do therapy."

A fun alternative is reading."

Bold of you to assume I can read."

Jupiter scowled. Do you want to keep that absolute dream of a man in your life or not, bitch?"

Emrys groaned, threw himself back on the pillows, put one over his face and proceeded to groan even louder. Why is caring about people so goddamn *hard*?"

Caring doesn't seem to be the hard part for you," Jupiter said, her voice muffled by the pillow Emrys kept affixed to his face. It's accepting other people's care that trips you up. It's like you're scared to even try being happy."

Emrys sat up, keeping his gaze on the pillow and playing with its fringe, brow furrowed. Bad things happen to people who care about me."

Jupiter studied him for a moment, then poured herself another shot. When I was in the 10th grade, Sammy's older sister took us to our first Pride. It was the first time I was brave enough to wear feminine clothes. I thought my dad was still on the night shift at his job, so he wouldn't be at the house when I got home. I was wrong. Do you know what happened when I walked in wearing a dress and a face full of makeup?"

He...yelled at you?"

Jupiter threw back her shot. He slugged me right in the mouth. Knocked out a tooth."

O...Oh."

But when I went down, instead of curling up and taking it, I tripped that bastard, kicked him right in the groin with my pointed heels and ran like hell. Probably wouldn't be here right now if I hadn't."

Emrys opened his mouth to respond, to ask why she was sharing this, but all he could settle on was, I'm so sorry."

Jupiter shrugged. That cock-face had it coming." She leaned forward, placing her bony elbows on the table and staring into Emrys' eyes, refusing to blink. Bad things are always going to happen, Emrys. That's part of life, especially if you're different, but they don't get to win. Not if you get up, kick them in the nuts, and fight like hell for the life you want."

Emrys looked away, dropping his gaze to his empty mug. What if that life isn't something I deserve? What if I'm not good enough for it?"

Emrys, you beautiful dumb bitch." Jupiter lifted his chin, a gentle, exasperated smile on her face. What if you are?"

Emrys' throat tightened, swearing he could hear his mother's cadence in Jupiter's voice. (Though, maybe not in the beautiful dumb bitch" part.) He gently pulled away and rubbed at his eyes. If you're going to psychoanalyze me, at least bring out the tarot cards and film it for your channel."

Jupiter leaned back in her beanbag and laughed. "Your concern for my business ventures is very touching." She checked her watch, eyebrows pulling together. "I hate to kick you out, but my boss is on ˹ their way, and I assume you don't want to explain what you're doing here. It would be a really awkward way to kick off Valentine's Day."

Emrys took his mug and exited the fort. Once properly on his feet, he stretched, taking in the crisp winter morning that bathed the store in daffodil light. Jupiter followed him and offered to take his mug.

"Let me put these down, and I'll unlock the front to let you out. *Properly.*"

Emrys chuckled, then began to meander, studying the shelves he had missed before. A small platform on a shelf caught his eye. Small, nondescript wooden figurines grabbed his attention on another. His chest lit up with the spark of an idea.

"Can I buy something first?" he called.

"Sure," Jupiter replied. "Grab it and meet me at the register."

She joined him at the counter, a ring of keys in one hand as she tapped the register's computer system awake.

As she scanned Emrys' purchases, he bounced on his feet, nervous to ask his next question. "Could you maybe wrap it?" He tossed his wallet from hand to hand. "It's a Valentine's Day present. For Zack."

Jupiter stopped mid-scan to give Emrys a tired look. "What did we just—"

"It's not an 'I'm being an absolute thot' present. It's an 'I'm *sorry* for being an absolute thot' present."

Jupiter chuckled and finished the transaction. "I'll get you a decorative bag."

"When you're done, let me put my number in your phone," Emrys said. When Jupiter gave him a quizzical look, he added, "If your coven comes across something that you're unfamiliar with or makes you uncomfortable, I want you to reach out. I don't care what time it is or where I am."

Jupiter almost laughed but stopped. "You're serious?"

Emrys massaged the back of his neck. "I was too hard on you the other day. You're doing your best to take care of Sammy and Stone with the cards stacked against you." He met Jupiter's eyes, pleading for her to forgive him for being so harsh. "Let me make it a little easier."

Jupiter beamed as she handed over her phone.

Emrys squirmed under the silent praise and dropped his gaze to the New Contact screen. Don't make me change my mind."

Jupiter chuckled as she rang up the purchase. It's okay." She handed back the phone. I had to start with baby steps, too."

Zackary's afternoon passed by in a muted haze. He texting Emrys to call for a ride when he was done with the glamours, then he lost himself in an internal storm of his own making as he sat in the lobby of Glace's medical clinic.

Why did he always have to do this? He shouldn't have pushed Emrys into dealing with his powers, and he shouldn't have pushed him into being more than whatever they were, because now what were they? Was Emrys right? Was Zackary trying to love the shit-show out of him and make him something he wasn't?

Zackary shook his head as he held it in his hands. No. He'd told the truth—he wanted *Emrys*, not some cleaned up, polished version that was supposedly "good enough."

But Emrys didn't want anything at all. He had made that abundantly clear.

Emrys never texted back and Zackary began to worry. He knew that he was safe, but Zackary feared that there was a real possibility that

Emrys wouldn't come back at all. It's not like he *had* to. He owed Zackary and Maryam nothing, he had gotten what he wanted, and the forest around Glace would more than fulfill the requirements of the bargain they had initially struck four months ago. Maybe Emrys had already found a new little corner of the woods to make his own or some fae or another to shack up with.

And maybe that was for the best. Maybe this was the only way this back-and-forth torment could end. Zackary almost wondered if he should be grateful—no more temptation, no more teasing. No more heartache.

Yet, instead of going to bed relieved, he tossed and turned all night and nearly flew out of bed the next morning at the smell of crackling bacon, nearly putting his clothes on backwards in his rush to get downstairs.

He stopped short on the landing, struggling to process the alien sight of Emrys at the stove, an apron down his front and a spatula in his hand. Emrys froze, his mouth opening and closing several times before he found the right words.

"These pancakes are plain," he said. "You used up the last of Gracie's chocolate chips."

Zackary wanted to laugh, but he only smiled, afraid to spook Emrys and send him running. "That's fine. Plain pancakes are good too."

Emrys nodded, then flipped the wonky cake onto the stack beside him. "I'm not as good at this as you are."

"There's a learning curve to it."

Emrys ladled more batter into the pan, his gaze locked intensely on the stream as he said, "I got you something for Valentine's Day."

Zackary blinked, then did a double take at the red paper bag in the center of the kitchen table, surprised that he hadn't noticed it with the red tulle bow on top. "O-oh." He looked at Emrys, who was still watching the stove, then back at the table before crossing the kitchen and delicately rummaging through the pink tissue paper.

He pulled out his present a piece at a time—first the small, polished wooden platform, then the faceless wooden figurines, two tall and slender with long flowing hair and three smaller ones, like children. A faint floral scent caught Zackary's nose. He poked his head in the bag to find three candles, one lavender, one chamomile, one wildflower.

He looked over the assembly spread over the table, then back to Emrys. "What is this?"

"It's an altar for your family." Emrys flipped the pancake, then turned and leaned against the counter, his arms folded as he toed a crack in the linoleum. "You said you hate Valentine's Day because you only get to share it with Maryam." He shrugged, gaze still down. "I thought maybe you'd appreciate having the rest of them close." He stole a glance at Zackary with a small, sheepish smile. "You're a dirty pagan now, after all."

Emotion welled in Zackary's throat as he struggled to find the right words to convey how much it meant that Emrys had not only listened but truly *heard* him.

Instead, all he managed was, "I never said pagans were dirty."

Emrys shook his head with a chuckle as he checked the pancake and set it on the stack. "It's also an apology present." He scraped the rest of the batter from the mixing bowl, spreading it as best he could before speaking again. He turned to Zackary, wringing his hands, brow furrowed as he said, "I'm sorry for all the cruel things I said yesterday. You didn't deserve any of them—"

Zackary shook his head. "I'm the one who should be sorry. I kept pushing you and—"

Emrys held up a hand to stop him. "Just let me finish, okay?"

Zackary shut his mouth as Emrys wrung his hands.

"It's not only that I'm sorry for. I haven't been fair to you since day one. Regardless of what we may or may not feel for each other physically, I haven't treated you with the respect you deserve for all the kindness you've shown me. I've made you uncomfortable and discounted your feelings."

Panic curled in Zackary's stomach. "Don't tell me you're leaving."

Emrys shook his head. "Not if you don't want me to—"

"I don't."

"—But I would like to start over as friends." Emrys swallowed hard. "Just friends." He twirled the spatula in his hands. "I think I need...friends right now. This whole debacle has shown me that I have a lot of things to work on. I need to stop trying to use flings and sex to hide from that. You don't deserve to be used like that."

The words should have been a relief. Zackary should have been proud of him. Hell, he *was* proud, but the words were like a sucker punch. Why were friends" all they could be? Emrys could work things out while Zackary romanced him and fawned over him.

Fell in love with him.

But this wasn't about him, so he smiled and began to place the pieces of his gift back in the bag. "Of course. I'd like nothing more."

Emrys gave a sheepish smile, then turned to tend to the last pancake.

Zackary waited, desperate for Emrys to say so much more as he stood there, his Valentine's present in his hand. He inched towards the stairs, taking the slowest, smallest steps of his immortal life.

"Zackary?"

The demon whirled. "Yes?"

Emrys blinked, as if caught off guard by Zackary's eagerness. He shook off the shock and smiled. "I just wanted to say thank you."

"Oh...for what?"

Emrys shrugged. "Everything, I guess. Letting me crash with you and Maryam, giving me a job. Not being afraid of me when I lost my hold on my power."

"Emrys..." Zackary ran his hand over his hair, struggling to find the right words—words that told Emrys the truth, but not too much of the truth. Words with the kindness and comfort Emrys needed right now. He sighed and settled on, "You're welcome." He studied Emrys for a long, quiet moment, wondering if the pixie could sense the unsaid words in the way Zackary watched him. "And I could never be afraid of you. You're..." Zackary swallowed the words he wanted to say and replaced them with, "You're very dear to me—the dearest pain in my ass I've ever had."

A glimmer caught in Emrys' eye as he smirked, something Zackary couldn't quite place.

He didn't need to. He needed to let it go.

Because that was what Emrys needed.

He cleared his throat and motioned to the bag. "Thank you for this. It's probably the most thoughtful Valentine's present I've ever received."

Emrys grinned, brightening the whole room. "Good. I was worried it wouldn't be fancy enough."

Zackary snorted. "Trust me, it's more than fancy enough. Last year Maryam got me a mug that said, 'Nobody Knows I'm in the Illuminati.' I still don't quite get the joke, but she thinks it's hilarious."

Emrys chuckled.

Zackary started back up the stairs. "I'm going to go pack this before breakfast."

"Of course." Emrys turned to remove the last pancake from the heat. "Check if Gracie is up, will you?"

Zackary didn't have to check. Gracie met him in the hallway, her brow furrowing when she read something on Zackary's face that he hadn't intended to share.

"Is he okay?"

"He seems so." Zackary motioned down to the kitchen. "He's making breakfast right now."

"What time did he get in?"

Zackary sighed and massaged his eyes. "No idea. He was down there when I got up." He opened his eyes to find Gracie giving him a sad, sympathetic smile. "What?"

"Regardless of what he told you, you should tell him how you feel."

Zackary shook his head. "That's not what he needs right now."

"And what about you?"

Zackary scoffed. "Bad things tend to happen when demons decide they have 'needs.'" Gracie frowned. Before she could argue, he slipped past her, rolling up the figurines in their tissue picture and placing them as gently as he could in his backpack.

Breakfast was pleasant. Gracie praised Emrys' cooking, and he wiggled uncomfortably under the compliments. Gracie shot Zackary knowing looks over her coffee mug, all of which he ignored.

With the dishes washed and their bags packed in the car, Zackary threw a stick for Zeus and Odin from the porch one final time before trying to shake Gracie's hand, only for her to pull him into a hug and whisper, "Sooner or later, you've got to tell him."

Zackary pulled away with a roll of his eyes. "Goodbye, Gracie."

The old woman laughed as she pulled Emrys into an extra-long, extra-tight hug. "You boys will always have a place here if you need it. Take care of yourselves. And don't take any shit from those old farts at the Order."

Emrys laughed as he gently pulled away. "Oh, don't worry. I won't." He smirked at Zackary. "And I'll make sure he stops taking their shit."

Zackary hopped down the stairs, hands in his pockets as he headed toward the car, wishing that he didn't have a flirty comeback in mind for Emrys' comment. Emrys joined him a moment later, settling into his seat and buckling his belt as Zackary turned on the car and backed out onto the road.

The radio did nothing to ease the awkward silence that settled over the car. Emrys drumming along to the beat on his thighs didn't help either, but that didn't stop him from trying.

"Soooo...home," he said.

"Yep," Zackary replied.

"What are we going to tell Maryam?"

Zackary pursed his lips into a tight line as he thought it over. His goddaughter had grown rather invested in his and Emrys' "situation-ship," as she liked to call it, but this...this was too much to discuss like some sort of gossip column, even if the person asking was close.

"I'll let you decide what to tell," Zackary finally said. "I think it's safe to say this trip took more out of you than it did out of me, emotionally speaking."

"I don't know what you're talking about." Emrys voice was laced with sarcasm. "I've never been so emotionally stable in my life."

"If you left that statement as *I've never been emotionally stable*, I would be inclined to agree with you."

Emrys lightly punched him in the arm. "Is this what friendship with you is like?"

"Unfortunately, yes," Zackary answered. "Want to back out?"

Emrys went quiet for a moment—too quiet for Zackary's liking. Just as he began to tense for fear that Emrys might say yes, the pixie said, "If you'll have me, I'll stay."

Something in the small, nervous tone of Emrys' voice twisted Zackary's heart. "Of course I will."

"Good." Emrys settled deeper into his seat, pulling his coat tighter around himself. "Because moving in the middle of winter would be a bitch and a half."

Zackary snorted and fiddled with the radio, grateful that some layer of normalcy had returned. He turned the volume up as he settled on a rock station, desperate for some sort of distraction from the fact that nothing would ever truly be normal again.

Not really.

Emrys fell asleep on the drive to the airport, then at the gate, only to be nudged awake to board. He'd been ready to doze right back off (he couldn't be afraid of a fiery metal death if he was asleep), but Zackary passed him a plastic airport gift shop bag.

Emrys looked it over once his belt was buckled. "What's this?"

"Your Valentine's Day present." Zackary stuffed his backpack under the seat in front of him. "Well, half of it. You're also off the schedule tonight."

Emrys rummaged through the bag, digging out a blue T-shirt. On it, a stick figure bird stood on a beach, his face beakless and the missing body part sticking in the sand. Framing the image were the words *Lake Superior: So Cold You'll Freeze Your Pecker Off*. The bag still held weight, so he gave it a shake, dropping a bag of red and white jellybeans onto his lap.

In spite of himself, in spite of everything, Emrys laughed, the sensation reaching deep in his chest, reminding him that the heart within was still beating.

"This is horrible." He wiped a tear from his eye and shoved the shirt back in the bag. "This shirt is ugly as sin." He studied the jellybeans. "And did you ever look to see what flavors were in here?"

Zackary beamed back. "I only told you the noble reasons I don't like Valentine's Day." He clicked his belt. "I forgot to mention that I'm also just terrible at picking gifts."

"I'm cutting this into a crop top once it's warm enough." Emrys ripped open the bag of candy. "Then maybe I'll *consider* wearing it." He popped a handful in his mouth, savoring the blooming mix of cherry and coconut on his tongue, and offered the bag to Zackary. "I feel like I need an equally horrible ratty ball cap to go with it."

Zackary laughed too, cupping one hand for the candy. "It would certainly be a look, provided you're not at work."

"Oh, I'm absolutely wearing that outfit to work."

The cargo holds below the plane banged shut, making Emrys flinch.

Zackary stopped chewing. "Do you need to hold my hand—"

"No." Emrys kicked himself for how quickly he had answered and the way the word had shaken. But when he met Zackary's gaze, the demon didn't seem to catch the weight behind it—the fear that, if Emrys touched him for even a moment right now, he might spill everything.

Emrys forced a smile and slipped the plastic bag with the shirt in his backpack. "No, I'm okay." He zipped up the pack and settled into his seat. "After this weekend, the thought of plummeting out of the sky and dying in a jet-fuel inferno doesn't scare me as much."

One of their neighbors did a double take toward Emrys. The panic on the man's face made it clear that, while he hadn't started his morning with that particular fear, he most certainly had it now.

Emrys watched as Zackary fought back a grin from the fear playing out over the man's face. Zackary then looked back at Emrys, his green eyes calculating and kind. "You know I'll always catch you, right? Even if we're facing a jet-fuel inferno."

Emrys' heart skipped a beat. He shifted, looked away from Zackary, and tapped the screen in front of him awake to scroll through the movies. "Of course. That's what friends do."

Emrys noted the way the Zackary paused but pretended not to, allowing the demon to settle into his seat for the flight as the attendant began his safety demonstration.

Emrys' eyes grew heavy as the plane took off. He lost his battle to keep them open as the plane reached cruising altitude, succumbing to exhaustion like he'd never known.

But just before he went under, he felt a brush, a hesitant nudge, and then the warmth of Zackary hooking their pinkies together.

ACKNOWLEDGMENTS

Thank you, as always, to those who travel with me through the weeds of bringing a story to life. Tulip—you always know just how to challenge me and continue to teach me to trust myself more than you'll ever know. Kari—you're still the greatest hype woman ever.

Mandy and Karin—I don't even know if you were tracking that this book was coming out, but I'm just always so glad to be doing this author thing with you two.

To the editing team at Keele Publishing, thank you ever so much for making this story shine!

And to all those staring down the next four years like the barrel of a gun, I'm right there with you. Breath, keep active, build community, and love yourselves. We got this.

Maryam Bishop stood alone and unafraid.

Well, she crept along the soggy forest floor alone and unafraid. Zackary had eliminated everyone else in the game—Wendy when the ping of her phone gave away her hiding place and Emrys shortly after when he provided a distraction for Maryam and Peter to make a run for it. Peter had been brave enough—or arguably, crazy enough—to try and take the demon on himself, weaving strikes in ways that used the demon's size and weight against him, but he, too, was ultimately taken down, the yellow strip of fabric ripped from the waistband of his pants, eliminating him from the game That left Maryam, who lay flat in the dirt behind a fallen tree. She peered through its rotted-out core, the sickly sweet smell of last autumn's leaves tickling her nose and the lazy April shower pelting her with fat icy drops that pushed her waterproof tracksuit to its limits and trickled down her neck.

The field appeared empty, except for the benches filed to face the looming crosses that looked over the lake, forming a shapeless chapel for campers or small groups that rented St. Mary's Interdenominational Retreat Center and Camp Grounds to bond.

Maryam snorted. "Bonding," her ass. These "bonding" trips were weekends where Zackary hazed the shit out of all of them with endless drills, sparing, survival training, meditation, and pop quizzes on the occult. She had to begrudgingly admit that they were all getting better, though. Wendy had actually remembered to use her blessed salt to give herself a chance to run, and Peter had actually managed to draw his dull sparing knives. Emrys had actually managed to knock the wind out of Zackary before he was taken out of the game. When they had had first started playing Capture the Saint, the rounds only lasted about ten to fifteen minutes. Twenty, if they all all hid first. Maryam glanced at her watched and realized with a bit of awe that they were forty minutes in and she actually just might snag a win.

She surveyed the field again, then eyed the small figure at the top of the center cross. Despite the enhanced eyesight that came with being half-demon, Maryam couldn't be quiet sure which saint it was. Francis, maybe? All the statues of pious men in robs, hands up and eyes downturned, had blended together. Truth be told, the identity of the saint didn't really matter—swiping it from its pedestal and getting it back to the retreat center before Zackary got to her, did.

Maryam lifted herself into a crouch and slowly crept along the tree-line, disturbing as few leaves and branches as possible. One snapped and she froze, whipping around to check her surroundings. No sign of Zackary. She set off again, lower and with more caution, holding her breath.

Branches to her right rustled. Maryam dove behind a tree stump. Slowly, ever so slowly, she lifted herself up to peak over the rotting wood to find nothing.

Zackary's voice skittered across her left ear.

"I keep telling you—keep your head on a swivel."

Maryam dropped one hand to the yellow slip in her waistband and thrusted the other elbow back, aiming for what she hoped would be Zackary's diaphragm. It hit lower in his gut, drawing an surprised *oof* from the demon as he scrambled to reach for Maryam's slip. Maryam grabbed hold of him, planted her feet, lifted and twisted, putting Zackary on his back before taking off into the skies.

She winced as her wide, white wings struck branches and twigs, but she flew hard nonetheless, blocking her face with her arms until she was clear of the trees and banking for the crosses. She pumped her wings harder, holding her body as tight and straight as an arrow, hands outstretched. A hand brushed her sneaker. She tucked her wings and dropped, forcing Zackary to course correct as she shot back up, zooming up the length of the cross and snatching the figuring from its perch. Maryam gave a hoot of victory as she continued upwards into the air, banking right towards the retreat center—

Except Zackary hadn't had time to stop before she turned.

Stars danced in Maryam's blurred vision as her godfather body collided with her, sending them both tumbling into the icy lake below. The shock of stabbing cold didn't help, forcing all the air from here lungs as she flailed to untangle herself and figure out which way was up. She spread her arms and thrashed towards the brighter shade of gray. Breaking the surface, she gulped down air and coughed, pulling her heavy mess of red curls from her face and slicking it back with both hands.

Both *empty* hands.

Zackary emerged, shaking his strawberry blonde hair form his face, one hand raised in triumph with Maryam's yellow strip in his grip He wiped the water from his face and studied his goddaughter as he treaded water. "I'm sorry, Maryam. I didn't mean to hit you that hard. I wasn't expecting you to stop like that. Are you okay?"

Maryam scowled. "No, I'm not. We lost." She tightened her jaw so her teeth wouldn't chatter. She already sounded a bit pathetic—shivering would only make it worse.

Zackary gave her a beaming smile as if it didn't matter, because of course it didn't matter to *him*. He always won. "You all did much better, though. I'm impressed you managed to throw me with that short of notice. You should be proud of yourself."

"I'll be proud when I actually win."

Zackary frowned. "That's not the point of these exercises." He shivered, bringing his arms around himself. "Let's get out of this water. It's colder than a witch's tits in a brass bra."

Maryam rolled her eyes. "*Anyone's* tits would be cold in a brass bra. And we can't go back in just yet. I lost the statue."

Zackary shrugged and began to swim for shore. "Don't worry about it. It was St. Anthony. If he's meant to, he'll find his way back."

Maryam chuckled as she kicked against the water. "You don't actually believe that, do you?"

Zackary smirked over his shoulder as he swam.

"Zack? Zackary. C'mon. Tell me you don't believe that."

He didn't answer. Maryam followed, watching as their friends sprinted out of the woods and across the field.

Peter reached them first, offering a hand as Maryam pulled herself from the water. "Are you okay?" He hovered beside her as she dragged herself across the thin strip of pebbly beach to the grass. "Are you hurt?"

"I'm *pissed,* but I'm fine," Maryam answered, wringing out her jacket. "I had the damn statue in my hand, got too cocky, and Zackary slammed into me when I tried to turn. I'm sorry."

Peter gave her an exasperated smile that lit up his dark eyes. "It's fine, May. That's the longest we've lasted. We'll get it next time."

May. That nickname had a way of making Maryam shiver when Peter said it. It had started with Emrys calling her "Maryam May," no matter how many times she told him her actual middle name, and had caught like wildfire. Wendy called her that just as often as Peter and Emrys, but something about the word wrapped in Peter's voice got it tangled up in her bones, weaving between her ribs.

It screwed with her head—the way he still wanted to be around, even though she had turned him down romantically. People didn't do that, did they? Hell, when she was growing up, people hardly tried to even be nice to her, so to have someone not only want to date her, but to still value her as a friend, even after she said no, still felt alien after all these months.

Wendy panted as she caught up to her brother, slowing to a stop and scowling down at her phone. "I could have stayed in longer if Mom hadn't texted me." She sucked on her teeth in annoyance. "She acts like turning seventeen doesn't mean anything."

"That's because it don't," Peter argued. "If turning seventeen helped you would have left that damn phone back at the retreat center like I told you."

Wendy glowered, simmering in silent angst.

Emrys passed the siblings and placed his arm around Maryam's waist, guiding her across the field. "We can debrief once we're inside, clean, and dry. No one's winning anything if the mortals get sick. We'll come back out and do better next time."

"No one's trying anything else tonight." Zackary sloshed up the bank, his sneakers squeaking as they leaked water. "It's getting dark. Time to clean up and make dinner."

Wendy's eyes lit up. "Can we eat around a campfire?"

Zackary shrugged. "Sure, provided we clean up afterwards."

Wendy gave him a wounded look as the group began to migrate across the field, back towards the retreat center. "I always clean up after myself."

Peter snorted. "Tell that to your room."

Wendy punched him in the arm.

Maryam stayed beside Emrys as the group walked, Wendy launching into a million questions for Zackary while Peter listened in. She glanced down to check on him, because she always felt the need to check on him these days, and noticed the way he watched the wet fabric cling to Zackary's broad, muscular shoulders and the taper of his waist.

Emrys was like that more often than not, now—watching and weighing Zackary's actions, the ways he carried himself and his words, but he hadn't made a single flirtatious comment since he and Zackary had returned from their team mission back in February.

Zackary refused to talk about whatever had happened. He said it wasn't his story to tell, so Maryam was left to prod Emrys as gently as possible, because she *would* figure out what the hell had happened between the two of them.

And what had happened to Emrys.

"You doing okay?" she asked.

"Hm?" Emrys blinked and smiled up at Maryam. "I'm fine. Just lost in thought."

Maryam glanced towards Zackary, then back at Emrys with a knowing smirk.

Emrys rolled his eyes. "Not about Zack."

"Em. Come on. Seriously. You can't hold out on me for ever."

Emrys sighed and folded his arms. "I can if there's nothing to tell." He looked away. "Why are you so convinced that I can't have a mature, adult relationship with someone I was once trying to sleep with?"

"Because you still turn to me and say, 'Nice,' whenever a customer's order ends in 69 cents."

Emrys snorted. "Like I didn't learn that from you."

"You're a hundred and fifty years old. I shouldn't be able to influence you so easily." Maryam studied Emrys as he shook his head and continued to walk, gaze now carefully schooled down on the path ahead of them, hands in the pockets of his mud-streaked joggers.

The lack of flirting with Zackary wasn't the only reason Maryam had been worried about Emrys. The second they had walked into Ectoplasm after their weekend, Maryam had known something was wrong. Emrys had been pale and somber, dark circles ringing his azure eyes that were normally sparkling with mischief. He'd given Maryam a peck on the cheek as way of greeting, then headed straight up stairs for a shower and a nap, taking the heavy cloud of sorrow with him.

Maryam had looked from the stairs to Zackary in bewilderment. "Is something wrong? Did the killer get away?"

Zackary's mouth had pressed into a hard line, his brow pulling down with the effort of keeping the truth at bay. "No. She's dead."

"Then what's the problem? Did she kill someone else?"

"No." Zackary had sighed, set his suitcase beside the bar, and then slid into a seat. "It was somethone Emrys knew. And he was the one that ended her." He had massaged his temples, eyes down on the counter and distant. "Get me a Gentleman Jack, will you?"

Maryam blinked, her mind reeling and her stomach rolling at the idea of either of them making a choice like that. They'd only been sent to find and arrest whatever supernatural entity had killed too human boys. What had gone so wrong that they had to kill her? What had gone so wrong that *Emrys* had to kill her?

But Maryam hadn't been able to ask any of that. She didn't know if she even wanted the answers just then, so instead she had just said, "It's nine a.m. on a Sunday, Zack."

Zackary had snorted, fingers still rotating against the sides of his forehead. "Oh, my mistake. Make it an Irish Coffee, then. Espresso. No whipped cream."

That had been the next sign that something was very, very wrong. Michigan state law said they weren't allowed to serve alcohol before noon on Sundays and Zackary had never once tried to cut a corner when it came to Ectoplasm. Maryam had still made the drink, but a nervous energy had thrummed beneath her skin the entire time, her fingers drumming impatiently as the espresso dripped from the machine and her toes tapping as the milk took entirely too long to steam.

She'd brought it back with a criss-cross pattern of salted caramel syrup on top and leaned on the counter as she placed it in front of her godfather. "What the hell happened out there? Is Emrys okay?"

Zackary had taken a long, deep sip with his eyes closed. When he sat the mug back on its saucer, he kept his eyes down. "I don't think it's my story to tell. And no." His grip on the mug handle tightened. "I don't think he's okay, but...Just given him time."

She had given him time, but here they were, two months later, and Emrys still hadn't said a word about the mission. He seemed to have gotten a little bit better. He laughed and joked again. He came girls' night with Maryam and Wendy and seemed to have fun, but in the quiet moments, Maryam could still feel the sadness radiating off of him. She still spotted a shadow in his eyes and a weight pressing down on his brow whenever he was left alone with his thoughts.

Worst of all, there was peace between Zackary and Emrys now. No arguing or banter. No electric tension that Emrys savored and Zackary fervorously denied. From the outside looking in, they seemed to be good friends, coworkers, and roommates, but Maryam could sense something had shifted between, as if the spark between them had burned through their bond and fizzled out, dead and cold.

Maryam wouldn't tell them but she hated it. It felt wrong. Sad.

Emrys linked his arms with Maryam's, holding tight and snuggling against her bicep. "I'm alright, love." He took her hand and kissed the back. "Truly."

Mayam took her arm back so that she could squeeze him, hoping to communicate that she was here if he ever needed her. Faeries couldn't lie, but that didn't mean they were particularly truthful. Maryam had learned the hard way that the truth had a bad habit of coming forth in its own time, whether folks liked it or not. People could work with or against it, but it would arrive all the same if it saw fit, damn the damage it left in its wake. All she could do was stand by and hope that Emrys' truth didn't kill him.

Because Maryam's truths had *almost* killed her.

Back at the retreat center, folks split off to clean up, the boys heading to their own rooms while Wendy and Maryam made their way to the room they shared. It had been Wendy's idea to bunk together, claiming that it would save time on the last day when they cleaned up to leave, and who would wake Maryam when she inevitably slept through her alarm?

Maryam had three other people who could wake her up (because she did have a bad habit of oversleeping), and cleaning the rooms never took long, but she let Wendy stay either way. She'd been through a lot for a sixteen year old—seventeen, now, as she loved to remind everyone. As if her father passing and her brother moving out to start his own life hadn't been enough, Wendy had accidently brought home an occult artifact tethered to a demon that had possessed her brother, nearly getting him killed. In the time since then, Maryam had learned Wendy's habits and tells as they spent more time together. If she wasn't feeling guilty for what had happened, she was watching over her shoulder for things that went bump in the night. As someone who had grown up with exorcist as legal guardians, Maryam couldn't blame her for being skittish in the dark now. Besides, it felt nice to be needed. To feel like a protector and savior after growing up feeling like a disaster and a curse.

"Rock, paper, scissors for the shower?" Wendy asked, unlacing her shoes. "You essentially just took a bath anyway."

Maryam peeled off her water-logged jacket and whipped it at her with a smirk. "Smart ass."

Wendy squealed against the impact of heavy, wet clothing, then threw it back. After a moment, she said, "I'm sorry we lost the game."

Maryam shrugged as she grabbed her towel. "Don't sweat it. I'm just a sore loser."

Wendy chewed her bottom lip for a moment. "We'll get better, you know," she blurted. "We won't always be like this."

Maryam paused, looking at the younger girl with a raised eyebrow. "Won't always be like what?"

Wendy picked at a small cut in the palm of her hand. "You know...Slow. Weak."

"Human" hung unsaid in the air.

Maryam crossed the space between them, taking Wendy's frigid hands in hers. "Wen, look at me."

Wendy lifted her gaze, brown knitted and eyes uncertain, still so very young, despite how hard Maryam knew she tried to prove she wasn't. Maryam studied the lines of her dirty palms, the smooth brown, untarnished plain of her inner forearms.

Maryam's had been so different at seventeen.

"You're exactly who and where you're supposed to be, kiddo," Maryam said softly. "You are not slow. You are not weak." She curled her fingers around Wendy's hands and gently squeezed. "You are brilliant and you are *learning*. That's all you need to do right now." She released Wendy's hands, brushing over the cut as she stepped away. "Clean that out and bandage it."

Wendy studied it, picking at the loose skin again. "It's not that bad."

Maryam shurged and stepped into the bathroom. "Alright, but don't say I didn't try to help when your brother tries to mama-hen you to death."

Wendy rolled her eyes and began rummaging through her backpack. "Good point. He definitely will. So annoying."

"Yeah, it's almost like he doesn't know you're *sixteen*."

Maryam dove for the bathroom and swung the door shut. She heard a soft *thud* and snorted in satisfaction as a flung pillow made contact with the wood. The old pipes clamored to life as she turned the knobs. She stripped off the rest of her soaked clothes and let the shower stream warm, moaning once she was under it as hot water chased away the chill and aches of the day.

It didn't matter how hard she trained between these trips or how much muscle she built, Zackary's trainings always kicked her ass. The thought made her scowl as she scrubbed along the hard lines of her body with a bar of vanilla soap. What was the point of being built like a bulldozer she still couldn't help her team win that stupid game? Or beat Zackary on a sparring mat? Or anything remotely remarkable like ankida'shi like her were apparently supposed to do? Given the way Zackary talked about all her half-demon kin, she should have been walking on water by now (which made her make a mental note to ask Zackary a particularly blasphemous question about Jesus later.)

Once clean and dry, Maryam cleared out of the bathroom, blow-drying and braiding her hair at the desk in the room so that Wendy could shower. The only person she could find in the entire center was Peter, who was in the midsts of packing a pair of wooden crates with campfire food and tools.

"The boys still cleaning up?" Maryam asked though the serving window.

"Just Zack, I think. Emrys already went out to start the fire." Peter answered, tossing a bag of marshmallows into the nearest crate. "Help me carry all this?" He flashed Maryam a smirk. "Unless you need me to carry both of them."

Maryam scoffed. "Fuck off, Bailey. I could carry both the crates *and* you."

Peter stacked the crates and picked them up with a wicked grin. "Bet."

"Don't you—Peter!" He launched himself into Maryam's arms, crates against his chest. Maryam scrambled to catch him, princess style, before he could fall on his ass. Sure enough, she held him aloft with relatively little strain. Peter's smaller frame helped, cut leaner in the months since he'd started training with Maryam and Zackary. Maryam secretly hated him for it a little bit—somehow the last four months had turned Peter into a garden variety twink while Maryam's already tall, athletic build had been filled out with muscle solid enough to take out a brick wall. Zackary pinned it on her ankida'shi genes. It made sense since he, too, was also built like He-Man and Hulk Hogan's love child, but it didn't make her feel any better.

Peter beamed up at Maryam, not the least bit insecure about the fact that could break him in half. Maryam wasn't sure whether it was his ease and comfort or the smile itself that made her face begin to heat. Instead of figuring it out, she turned away and eased Peter to the ground, taking one of the crates with her.

"You're so annoying," she grumbled.

"Nah, you love me." Peter shrugged and headed off towards the exit.

Maryam missed a step, then followed after him with a roll of her eyes. She couldn't decide whether she appreciated how easily Peter used the l-word or whether it meant he still held on to the possibility that they might be something more. He hadn't brought up dating again after asking while he was in the hospital following a demon nearly ripping him apart from the inside out. He didn't seem to think about that conversation at all, honestly, but Maryam couldn't shake the worry.

Maybe she needed to just let it go and enjoy the fact that she did, in fact, for the first time in her life, have not one, but multiple friends that loved her.

Maybe she needed to bring it up again. Maybe that would be stupid.

The two of them reached the fire pit before she could decided. Emrys sat on a curiously dry log cin front of a curiously healthy fire, despite the way water still dripped off twigs and leaves. He looked up at the sound of their approaching footsteps and grinned.

"Thank the gods. I was about to start chewing on bark to starve off the hunger." He began rummaging through the crates as Peter and Maryam set them down. "We packed those irons the let you make grilled, right?"

"Yeah, but doesn't iron make you sick?" Peter asked.

Emrys motioned to the a woven bracelet around his wrists. "That's what charms are for, darling."

The charms must have been the extra-strength kind, because Emrys had scarfed down two grilled cheese sandwiches by the time Zackary and Wendy joined. He, much like Peter, had gotten fit with the training, eating nearly as much as Maryam to fuel his efforts to keep up as the smallest of their party, but not showing any of it in bulk. Lucky bastard.

Zackary sat down next to him, handing him a beer from the six pack in his hand. "Were you planning on leaving any food for the rest of us?"

"Oh, fuck off," Emrys said around the last bite of sandwich. "We always pack like the world's going to end while we're out here. There's plenty." He popped the top off the beer and took a swig.

Wendy cupped her hands around a thermos of what Maryam figured was hot chocolate, looking over the contents of the crates, then selecting a protein bar. She eyed the six pack as her brother took a bottle. Peter stared her down, pointing to his own eyes, then to her face. She scowled at him. "What? I'm not doing anything."

"Good." Peter took the top from his drink. "Keep on not doing anything and we won't have any problems."

Maryam chuckled as she took her own grilled cheese from the fire, opened the two-sided griddle, and inspected her work—inside was a perfectly golden sandwich, making her mouth water. She removed it with her fingertips, mindful of the hot metal as she passed the tool to Zackary and took a bite. Salty butter, toasty bread, and rich, savoy cheese melted together in her mouth, warming her form the inside as she watched her ragtag group of...Maryam wasn't quite sure what to call them. All she knew was she was theirs, they were hers, and despite the aches and pains of the day, this moment was perfect.

Brush shivered nearby.

Zackary positioned himself between the sound and the group, Peter positioning himself in front of his sister and Emrys drawing a knife from his boot (which Maryam told herself to ask about later). As the furthest from the sound, she only watched, iron now shut over her sandwich in case she had to get up and bludon someone with her dinner.

A figure emerged from the dark, clad in leather armor streaked with blood, the tip of one pointed ear a gnarled, bloody mess. In the firelight, Maryam could make out a ornate, flourishing H against the man's chest, signalling that the man belonged to the Hemlock court. *Emry's* court. The faerie stumbled forward, clutching his chest as he tried to speak. Only a trickle of blood made it beyond his lips before his foot snagged on a root and he went to his knees.

The movement broke the spell of stillness. Emrys darted forward to catch the man before he could fall on his face, Zackary right behind him while Peter held Wendy back. Maryam got to her feet, but stayed rooted to the spot, dumbfounded with her brain short circuiting as she tried to make sense of what she was seeing.

Faeries didn't bother with other beings and Emrys didn't seem bother with them, for the most part. From what little he had told her over the months, anyone properly tied to the Hemlock court had orders to kill him on sight and bring his head to their queen. Whether they followed that instruction was hit or miss and Emrys, though lacking sense in plenty of departments, never seemed eager to play Russian roulette with his fellow goodfolk.

Nausea swirled in Maryam's stomach. What could be so terrible just beyond the firelight that a faerie would come not only to strangers, but to his court's bastard's prince?

"Slow down. Breathe," Emrys said softly, brushing the faerie's matted hair from his face. "What's happened?"

The man took a wet, wheezing breath. "Hemlock has fallen." He rose a hand passed Emrys' face, as if motioning to the ram horns that sat atop Emrys' head when his glamour was down. "Queen Maeve is...."

The faerie's arm dropped to the ground as the words died on his lips.

The only sounds left were the fire and the night.

FOLLOW ME ON SOCIAL MEDIA!

FINNELY.RAY   FINNELYRAY

FINNELYRAY
@GMAIL.COM

KOFI.COM/
FINNELYRAY

AUTHOR_FINNELY.RAY

SUMMON UPDATES, BEHIND THE SCENES CONTENT, AND MORE!